By The Blue Moon

Blue Moon Magic ~ Book 1

Debi Wilder

By The Blue Moon

By Debi Wilder

CreateSpace Edition

Copyright © 2007 Debi Wilder

Published by Shooting Star Books at CreateSpace
www.shootingstarbooks.com

Cover Art by Scott Carpenter,
P and N Graphics, Inc.
Edited by Alicia Dean
Proofreading and Formatting by
Jim and Zetta Author and Publishing Services

ISBN 10 ~ 1-62052-028-1
ISBN 13 ~ 978-1-62052-028-4

Discover other books by Author

Visit Debi at these places:
http://authordebiwilder.blogspot.com/
Follow author on twitter: @waMaxineDouglas

BLUE
MOON
Magic

Contents

Dedication

If not for my fellow Blue Moon authors and friends, Honey Jans, Sherry Dare and Lynn Crain, this series wouldn't be what it is today and has always been...filled with wonderful magic. I thank and love all three of you for being a part of it all.

To the people who live around the Kettle Moraine Forest in Wisconsin and have seen the beast that sometimes lurks among the trees, these stories are for you and all that you believe in. For you see, I believe in the unknown as much as you do.

To my husband who is always quick to let me know when things don't make sense, even if I do disagree with him from time-to-time, I appreciate you more than words could ever express.

To my new readers of the Blue Moon Series, I hope you enjoy the story of the Langfords and will be waiting patiently for the next set of stories to come out.

Hugs – Debi Wilder

Prologue

The light of the full moon shimmered through the vast window of Justin Matthew Sinclair's penthouse condo. Pacing the length of the condo only added to his nervous excitement. Charles Langford, leader of the Elite wolf clan, called and asked to see him. The urgency in his voice only meant one thing; the time had come for Justin to claim his mate.

Like the Langford girls, he'd been born to live the life of a wolfen. It was one of the reasons he'd left his native English township of Hillshire as a young man. When he was but three years of age, word came from their North American cousins he'd been promised the first she-wolf born from the union of Charles and Joanna Langford.

Justin flipped through the file containing his mate's information. Born thirty-four years ago, Chastity Langford showed signs of the prized strawberry colored hair even as an infant. Her perfect heart-shaped face and yellow-green eyes held the promise of a lust level known only to those who possessed the ancient she-wolf looks.

Even in the file's photographs, she held the power to cause his arousal to swell painfully against his pants. If she held sexual power over him now, what would it be like to see her in person? To hold her image in his eyes, inhale her scent, and feel the overwhelming desire to take her with a fiery need known only during the season of the blue moon?

It had been over a hundred years since a red she-wolf lived to take her rightful place in the clan. A red-haired princess brought the promise of a new day; a day when the beast men clan could come out of hiding and further their kind with human mates. The wolfen clan would throw caution to the full moon, with only the strong surviving.

A human mate wouldn't be enough to satisfy Justin. He'd been born for this time, to take the lead of the clan and guide the young wolves in the hunt for their mates during the ancient mating ceremony. Their mating would last more than a human lifetime for the wolfen clan and the humans they took as their life mates.

As the eldest of the Blue Moon Sisters, Chastity had been promised to him as she made her way from her mother's womb into the world. A world where a wolfen society survived among humans; living for the season of the blue moon. The rite of passage would soon take place, and Justin would claim his life mate, just as his ancestors before him. The thrill of the hunt, the risk, claiming his mate, vibrated through his soul. Would he live through it this time around?

Chapter 1

Her dress hiked up to her waist, she gripped the edge of the cool mahogany desk. Her breasts flattened against the dark richness of the desktop, her nipples pebbled with hard desire for his touch. His large, roughened hand moved softly over her garter-clad ass as a knee wedged her legs further apart—his flesh warm and hard through her black fishnet stockings. Her opening spread to accommodate the breadth of two long fingers that coaxed her juices to flow rapidly. She sucked in a whisper of a breath as he did his magic to her channel. Now, please take me now, *she silently pleaded, wanting nothing more than to feel him spank her butt cheek hard before claiming her. Her hips shifted with his movements...*

"Chas?"

Chastity Langford became rigid in her chair at the sound of her name, bringing her out of what had become one of her usual lunchtime fantasies. *Damn!* She opened her eyes and quickly gathered her composure before turning away from the vast window overlooking the

Jefferson River.

Her middle sister, Charity, stood just outside her office door. Her eyes rounded, her mouth hanging open in shock, like she'd just walked in on their parents. "The least you could do is close the blinds. I don't understand what's come over you lately." With an eye on the pathway along a row of cubicles, she made sure no one headed their way. "One of these days you're going to get caught in the midst of your erotic daydreams by Clarity and summoned right up to Daddy's door. You know how she is."

Chastity laughed, smoothing her skirt. "Playing with herself might make her ease up a bit, it certainly helps me. Anyway, I really think she needs to get laid or something. Maybe I'll buy her a vibrator that'll really put her over the sexual edge."

Charity stepped into the office, closing the door behind her. "She's our little sister, Chas. And even though you believe that's what she needs, the problem is she doesn't. You've got to respect her feelings and mine. Please try to understand them as well. And the truth be told, neither of us really understands what's happening either, Chas. If I were you, I'd plan on being very cautious from here on in."

Chastity knew in her heart Charity was right. Over the past few months, the idea of sex had started to distract her from business. All she could think about was finding out what it was like, and the more she read, the more she fantasized about it. The more her body craved to know what it felt like to have a man inside her, the more she found ways to imagine it happening. Like today, being caught with her hand between her legs, literally. Thankfully the little silver egg-shaped vibrator purred in silence, keeping her secret safe.

She looked across her desk at her sister, wondering why, now that she'd hit her thirties, she seemed to be enveloped in wanting to be screwed like a whore in the night. They used to be so alike, driven to succeed in business, not giving sex a second thought. Now she was randy as a bitch in heat, leaving Clarity and Charity the only ones who acted normal. As sisters, they'd always seemed to go through their stages together, but no more. They were as close to triplets, without being triplets, as was humanly possible, each born within a year of the other. Their parents certainly had a thirst for sex in their fertile years, even if there were no more babies born into the family.

"You and Clarity don't seem to be affected by this at all." She sighed deeply and turned back to the calm waters of the river. "I wish I had the answers to my sexual craving, Charity."

As the eldest daughter of a founding member of Langford and Langford, Chastity took her position seriously...overseeing the HR Department and protecting her younger sisters. It wasn't glamorous by any stretch of the imagination, but it gave her a sense of responsibility and self-worth. She'd earned the position, having majored in general business with a minor in human resources and narrowly beating out some of the top students in her class.

Over the past few months she'd found her mind wandering, and she spent hours daydreaming about nothing in particular. Only recently, thoughts of sex gave her more of a sense of power than the prospect of someday running a company built on sweat and tears, with an occasional spillage of blood that never hurt anyone. At least that's what Daddy and Uncle Foster kept telling her, and that's all they told her.

At thirty-four she still had no idea what really lay beneath the foundation of Langford and Langford. She had this unsettling feeling, for the moment, she was better off not knowing. She had more pressing matters to contend with, like getting back to her fantasy and the silver object still humming inside her.

"Oh, by the way, Mr. Matthews is asking for you. Something about you being late for a penthouse meeting, which, thankfully, I wasn't asked to attend." Charity winked then walked out of the office while Chastity hustled to button the opening in her dress and apply a fresh coat of lip gloss.

***

Chastity strolled into her father's penthouse office like a she-wolf on the prowl. *If only she knew how true to form she really is*, Justin laughed to himself, feeling the all too familiar ache of his hard-on. *I can only assume it was like this for all the Sinclairs when their mates were coming into heat for the first time. I could smell her juices before she walked through the door.*

If she knew the reaction her mere presence caused in his mind and body, she might not be so smug about being a Langford. Or maybe she would; after all, she was the prized possession of the Langford clan. The eldest of the Blue Moon Sisters, as the clan referred to them, to carry on their ancient lineage...and his.

Since being brought in to the company by Charles Langford, he took liberties. His high ranking place in the family business railed on the nerves of some. Chastity didn't have a clue as to why he was there. But she would soon enough, and he couldn't wait to be there when she did.

"Daddy." Leaning over she placed a kiss on her father's cheek, revealing a hint of cleavage.

Justin sat back, tapping his pen in annoyance as saliva seeped at the corners of his mouth. "You're late, Ms. Langford."

"Justin." Chastity took her place to the right of her father, a killer smile on her face that radiated sexual need. "Nice to see you too."

Damn! He nodded, pushing a stack of papers across the table. *It would be a lot nicer for both of us if you were bare-assed naked instead of suited up tighter than a Christmas present. As soon as possible, I'm going to unwrap that pretty little package.*

"Shall we get on with it?" Justin flipped open the first page. His crotch swelled as he watched her breasts strain beneath the fabric of her dress. He thought of nothing more than taking those pebbled nipples in his mouth. Noticing little things about her, he shifted to release the tension in his groin. He tried to slow his heart rate and swallowed back the dryness.

Her eyes yellowed deeper when she gave him that "go to hell" look. And her full lips pouted when she looked at her father. Damn she was a powerful woman and didn't even realize her potential. He took a deep breath hoping the surge of lust would come down to a quiet wave.

Justin leaned forward, the smell of her near orgasm penetrating his senses. He almost came with the knowledge that she'd been playing with herself again. "I promise to make things as easy on you as possible, Ms. Langford."

"Chastity," Charles Langford said, settling deeper in his chair. "I'll cut to the chase. From this day forward, you'll be working with Justin. The two of you will be together constantly. If this company is going to continue through the years to come, you'll have to do as I say...and as Justin instructs. I don't have time to listen to your objections. There isn't time, so don't even try."

Chas opened her mouth in what Justin presumed would be a major protest. He fully expected her to kick and scream all the way through this meeting. *Kicking and screaming could be a good thing, as long as she was at my mercy.*

Charles raised his hand to stop any protest Chastity might have given. "Listen to me, I said no objections and I mean it."

"Daddy, I don't need this...this watch dog with me day and night. HR isn't that exciting...in fact Charity or Clarity could handle it better than I."

"It's time to take your rightful place, Chastity." After getting up from his chair, Charles Langford stood behind Justin. "Your sisters' time will come. For now you will do as I instruct. Justin will be your guide and your mentor, follow him carefully. Justin, you have my blessing to do as you must. Being the eldest, Chastity will no doubt try to run rough shod over you."

"Yes sir, she'll be just fine." Justin captured his future mate's yellow-green eyes with his own. "It'll be a pleasure, I'm sure." In his human heart he knew he had a challenge sitting in front of him, but his wolf heart howled with anticipation of Chastity Langford's sweet nectar dripping on him.

***

Chas stiffened as her father left the meeting room. *What in the hell is Daddy thinking?* Part of her wanted to jump up and scream at the top of her lungs, while the other part found it a great opportunity to play with Mr. Justin Matthews. She'd have to think about the game to be played first. She contemplated a rousing game of strip *Monopoly* if for no other reason than to see if he had the balls to take on the challenge of getting her to do his bidding, but decided against it. She doubted he played fair at anything.

"I don't need your *guidance*, Justin. Least of all how to run the HR Department." Chastity licked her lips, pushing away from the table. The power of his sexuality took her by surprise, filling her body with a need to have him inside her.

Funny, she hadn't noticed her wanton thoughts while her father was in the room with them. Why now? Why all of a sudden did she become filled with a need to throw herself at the little pissant sitting smugly across the table? Even if she did find him attractive and wanted to find out what lay underneath the tight leather black pants, he was still a pissant who wormed his way into her father's good graces. A long-haired Adonis whose physical presence melted her into a pool of liquid silver.

Maybe jumping his bones wouldn't be such a bad idea. I'd finally find out what having the real thing instead of a pink rubber device would be like. Hell, on second thought, she wasn't up for that kind of rejection now or ever. Or at least not until she'd had a little more experience in the area of bodily pleasures.

Justin smiled, getting out of his chair and drawing in a breath. "Wow, so you do have a...bitchy side to you. I would never have guessed it the way you walked in here all prim and proper."

"You sure can be a prick when you want to be, Matthews." She stood and moved from the table, the need for distance warring with the need to be in his arms. He was so damn sexy.

Smirking, he picked up the stack of papers and walked toward her. "I have a feeling you like that quality in me, Ms. Langford."

"In your dreams, Mr. Matthews," Chastity spat, finding herself backed up against the vast span of glass. The papers he'd held fluttered around her feet.

With Justin standing mere inches from her, all she had to do was reach out and smack that smirk clean off his face. Instead, her feminine core quivered in anticipation of what his closeness may promise. She held his hot gaze, his gold-specked eyes reflecting the orange glow of the setting sun.

His hands moved lightly over her breasts then pinched a nipple hard and fast. A hot shiver seared through her and she licked her lips. She held fast as he pressed his bulging hard-on against her thigh, her clit twitching with need. Her inner muscles tightened around the silver object purring in her panties against her clit, her hot juices seeping from her.

Nearing the edge of coming in her silk undies, she closed her eyes slightly. *If he would only move a fraction of an inch to my mound, I won't be able to keep silent...or keep my hands off him. Come on Justin, just a little bit more. Show me what you've got to offer a woman, Matthews.*

As if he'd heard her plea, he pressed harder against the inside of her thigh. His fingers brushing against the outside of her breast, and she moaned with pleasure. His breath hot against her ear, she heard a whisper of words and sunk into him.

"Remember, my dear Chastity, I'm the one in control here. I'm a perfect match for that she-wolf instinct growing inside you."

She-wolf? He thinks of animals at a time like this? She quivered slightly, his tongue and teeth nipping at her ear lobe, followed by a soft growl. The sound sensual and powerful, she moaned with the wave of a liquid hot climax threatening to shudder through her body.

Breathless, Chastity focused to find herself alone with her dress unbuttoned, her panties pooled around her ankles, and one breast pulled from her white lace bra, its nipple held in a jeweled clip.

Chapter 2

"Damn!" Justin swore under his breath. "How can one woman hold that kind of sexual power?"

The image of Chastity with her dress wide open and legs spread apart with her panties pooled around her ankles brought him back to throbbing attention. Completely filled with lust and need, she hadn't noticed him slip the silk from her, exposing the small, humming vibrator nestled inside her. Her juices saturated his nostrils and sent his mating instincts into overload. If not for the device, he would have taken her then, not waiting to do so at the bonding ritual.

Instead, he settled for the feel of her soft breast in his hand and the way her nipple beaded at his touch. Her panting and willingness to open her body to him made marking her easier than he thought it would have been. On the verge of her coming, he'd pierced her nipple with a fang then slipped it into a blue star sapphire clip. If another tried to claim her, the clip would warn them whom she belonged too. The symbol was as ancient as the American wolfen clans, no one would dare to harm her.

The stone's color represented the blue moon while the star represented the marking between his eyes. The marking only visible to the wolfen clan, its faintness otherwise untraceable by the human eye. Only a wolfen's keen sense of sight would be able to detect the mark of the Sinclair family.

Having taken his middle name as his surname, Justin sometimes wondered if saving Charles had been a wise thing. Since that night, Charles had warned him not to go by his birth name, and one day, he'd understand why. If only that day would come so he could claim Chastity rightfully, rather than through deception.

"You'd better be careful, Justin. I smell my big sister all over you."

Justin stopped dead in his tracks, turning to find little Miss Clarity Langford inches from his back.

"You may be able to fool your big sisters, Clarity, but not the big bad wolf." *How in the hell did she manage to sneak up on me?* She was more human than wolf, unlike her sisters. The lust to mate pushed aside his senses. He must not be so careless in the days to come.

"Hell, Justin, my sisters have a long way to go before they can even begin to understand what's happening to them." She brushed past him. "I, for one, welcome that night to come. Then, finally, they both might stop making spectacles of themselves around here."

Snorting, Justin watched the youngest of the

sisters slink down the hall. If Charles knew the wild one he had in his youngest, he might find a suitable mate for her. One that would be strong enough to withstand her human nature. Just by her smell, Justin knew she was the third born into the family. He well remembered the stories told in his native land about the powers of the third born.

He'd been lucky enough to have his mate pledged to him as she came into this world. The Sinclairs were of ancient blood, like the Langfords. The mating of the two families would guarantee the survival of their kind, as it had always been and always would be.

***

Chastity tugged at the clip attached to her right nipple. Each time she pulled at the jewel a quick surge of pleasure raced through her.

"Damn it all any way!" Frustrated by her feeble attempts, she finally pulled the lace material up over her breast. "That son of a bitch. I'll kill him for this."

"You are a sight, dear sister." Clarity's laughing words pierced Chastity's heart. It wasn't so much what she said, but how she said it. The words had a ring of distaste to them.

"What the hell do you know, Clarity? You and your sweet little innocence can just turn around and go back wherever it was you came from," Chastity spat, shoving the dress buttons through their holes. The last thing she needed was her baby sister witnessing the brand laid upon her. So much for the saying of a little sister looking up to her big sister for moral guidance. What kind of an example was she setting for Clarity now?

Chastity glanced up to see her little sister, a smug smile across her face, still standing in the doorway.

"You still here?" *Please go away, Clari.* It wasn't fair to place her anger onto Clarity when it was really aimed at Justin and what he'd managed to do to her.

Clarity shook her head then pushed off the door jam. "That's some jewel you've got attached to your..."

Shit! "It's none of your concern, baby sister." Embarrassed as hell, Chastity walked over to the table, grabbing the papers scattered across it. She had to figure out a way to explain the item to Clarity, not to mention why it was clipped to her nipple and how it got there.

"That may be so, but I'll place a wager that Mr. Justin Matthews has something to do with your, ah, state of affairs." Clarity's voice came from mere inches behind Chastity's head. "Maybe you'll finally have a beast of a man to pleasure you, rather than doing it yourself. And one financially independent to boot."

Chastity spun around and slapped her sister across the face. As soon as her hand connected with the soft cheek, sorrow filled her heart. "Oh God! Clari, I'm sorry..."

Tears gleamed in Clarity's eyes, reflecting not only hurt but also anger. "If I were you Chas, I'd find a way to get rid of that sexual frustration you carry around, and fast."

She shivered, feeling the heat of fury in Clarity's eyes as she circled the table. She'd never hit another person in her entire life, now she'd hurt one of the people she loved more than life itself.

Heading for the door, Clarity stopped short. "You're forgiven this time, Chas. The next time, I'll rip your throat out," she warned, walking out the door.

Chastity sunk into one of the chairs. Her heart raced with the fear Clari's words left behind. Her little sister's eyes sparked red and venom spilled with the threat. Clari had a right to be upset.

She'd never in her entire life treated any of her sisters in the way she'd just done to Clarity. Yeah, she made fun of her little sister's innocence with Charity, but that was nothing more than sibling teasing. She'd never laid a hand on her sisters. Never even had cause to. They never threatened each other the way Clarity had just done.

Twilight filled the penthouse meeting room, but Chastity barely noticed. Her life was fast becoming a mess, falling deeper into the shit can, and she had to find some way of cleaning it up before more damage piled on top of it.

In the course of a few hours, she'd been handed over to that pissant Justin Matthews by her father, fully enjoyed being sexually manipulated by said pissant, physically assaulted her baby sister, and been threatened because of it. How was she going to face her family feeling she'd become less of the person who'd woken up this morning? Where in the hell had her pride and common sense disappeared too?

Smoothing her hand down her dress, Chastity unbuttoned a few buttons in the area of her mound. Reaching through the opening with her fingers, pulling the front of her panties down, she slipped her fingers through the folds...much like Justin had done not so long ago. Searching, she touched the smooth, humming object still nestled inside her...promising her pleasure if she'd only give in to it. Shutting her eyes, she slowly pulled the egg-shaped vibrator from its warm cocoon by the cord. She sucked in a ragged breath as it passed along her clit and lips. Without chancing a glance at the object of her lunchtime climaxes, she dropped it into the trash basket just inside the door.

***

Justin sank into the shadows of the dark hall as Clarity burst through the conference room doorway. He'd followed her, knowing she'd search her sister out. He couldn't help wonder if she'd done so to tease her about her sexual vulnerability rather than to check on her emotional condition. Being a bit curious himself about Chastity, he'd kept his distance and followed Clarity's scent.

By the sounds of things, she'd found Chastity in a less than respectable condition. Clarity's snarled threat raised the hair on his arms. If Chastity wasn't careful, she'd find an enemy in the family, and that would be anything but acceptable.

He'd have to figure out something to do to smooth the rift over. The three sisters had to work together; if not, the night of the blue moon would be lost and so would the clan. Their mating ritual relied on the sisters being together and in harmony, not at each other's throats...literally.

Clarity's footsteps fell heavy and fast on the carpet, every movement reflecting anger. She blew past him, snarling a warning to stay away from her. He responded in a low growl before moving deeper into the shadows.

Chapter 3

"Clari!" Chastity called out to the dark image rounding the corner. "Please wait...Damn it."

In the silence which followed the wake of her sister's shadow, Chastity walked slowly down the corridor. She needed to mend things with Clarity before their parents found out what had happened, because sure as shooting, Clarity would run to them with the news.

She still didn't understand why the teasing about Justin had pushed her over the edge of control. Granted, her sister's kidding around could be hard, and it had come at a bad time. Her father's sudden announcement of her working with Justin had fueled the fire, but it was still no excuse for her actions.

That was another thing she needed to get to the bottom of. Why would her father assign her to a person who barely knew anything about the company, much less a man who sent her wanton thoughts into overdrive? Her father couldn't possible know that unless...

"Crap." Someone had been spying on her,

she knew it. Who would have the nerve to tell her father about her masturbating during lunch? Furthermore, how would they even suspect unless... Clarity could have caught her in the act, but she wouldn't tell, would she?

Chastity shook her head, too many questions with too few answers. She wouldn't get any further without asking a few questions of her own, and she'd start with Justin Matthews as soon as she caught up to him.

"Looking for the big, bad wolf?"

"Holy shit, Justin." *Think of the Devil, and there he is. Where in the hell did he come from?* Chastity questioned in silence as she peeled herself off the ceiling. "You scared the hell out of me. Don't ever do it again."

"Sorry, I thought I'd heard you were looking for me." He stepped further from the shadows, his musky, sexual scent reminding her just why he had the power to send her body into a fiery need. "Or was I mistaken?"

If he steps any closer, I'm going to die right here, right now. Chastity swallowed hard, her heart pounding inside her chest. "I do need to ask you a few questions." *God, he's coming closer. Now what do I do...move or stand here like a bitch in heat waiting to be taken? Move. I've got to move...NOW.*

He stood so close to her she could feel the heat from his body. Her center quivered in response to his sheer presence, his sexual scent. Could it be he wanted her as much as she wanted him? Impossible. He was a pompous jerk who'd wormed his way into being a mentor she didn't want or need.

***

Chastity moved to the left and Justin blocked her with his right arm. She turned to face him, her eyes burning with fire...and fear. It was good that she feared him, she should. After all, he would be her mate for life. The one man she would never live without once the ritual took place.

Now that they were separated only by the width of their clothing, Justin's keen sense of hearing picked up nothing except her ragged breathing and the sound of her pounding heart. The smell of her panic mixed with the smell of her sex tempted his primitive mating senses. Damn but he wanted to take her in his arms, but it wasn't time for that right now. No silly, wonderful tenderness until he'd done what he needed to do. Once he made her his own and they'd become one, he'd curl her up next to him and hold her until the passing of the moon. Only then could they lead some resemblance to normalcy in a world where humans and wolfens cohabitated with each other.

Well, well, well. No little vibrating machine. She must have pulled it out after Clarity stormed out of the office. No wonder I can smell her juices so freely.

"Going so fast? I thought you had a question or two for me." He could feel her nipples jut out her breasts and harden lightly against him. They barely touched each other, yet her beaded nipples strained to reach him, begging to be

~ 22 ~

fondled. He licked his lips remembering how sweet and wonderful they'd tasted in his mouth only an hour ago.

Her head rested against the wall, exposing her delicate neck to him. Nestling her hair, its softness light and airy against his face, Justin lightly traced the edge of her ear with the tip of his tongue. "Come on, Chastity, what is it you want?"

He felt her quiver as her hand brushed past his rock hardness. "What I want is for you to stand over there," she panted, pointing to the opposite side of the hall. Her words said one thing, but her body was telling him something totally different. She wanted to get laid. And not just by anyone, but by him. It would only take strategically placed pressure and he'd be able to capture her where she stood.

Justin pressed against her, feeling his rod thump just above her mound. The musical sound of her mewing sent a wave of heat to his tip.

"If you insist, Chastity." He backed far enough to see the heat of desire on her face. He'd need all his wolfen powers to keep himself at bay. The need to mate grew stronger, and if he weakened, it would be over before it began.

***

Damn it! Chastity gave Justin a quick shove in the chest, moving him almost a foot away from her. "Don't you come near me, Matthews. I don't know what you've got up your sleeve, but be certain that I don't want any part of it." *Liar, liar pants on fire.*

His beautiful smile melted her resistance just a tad. "Now, Chastity, we both know that's impossible."

"Stop calling me that...you'll refer to me as Ms. Langford. And if you think for one moment that I'm going to abide by Daddy's command, you're sorely mistaken." *Even if I'd love nothing more than to feel your hardness inside me. Oh yeah, I bet you're big and... Damn it but that man gets under my skin!* She slid along the wall toward the elevator doors. Her left arm stretched against the coolness, she never took her eyes off his luscious body. With every inch she moved, he matched it with fluidness.

"As I remember it, your father said you had no choice in the matter. You were to do as I say, Ms. Langford." His eyes sparkled through the shadows, sending surges of desire through her core. If she were a little experienced, she fancied doing it in the hallway with him. Taking hold of his cock and...do what? Exactly! She wasn't about to embarrass herself with this man who smelled of experience and know-how in the ways of sex.

"Not like I've never gone against my father, Matthews." *Not unless I wanted my butt kicked around the block and back that is, but he doesn't need to know that.*

"Really? I doubt it, Ms. Langford. In fact I think you take instruction very well."

Chastity exhaled the breath she'd been holding as her fingertips slid over the elevator button and she pressed it. She'd be able to escape him as soon as the elevator came. "Do you want to press your luck, Matthews? Or are you going to take my word as truth?" *Come on damn it!* She pressed the button again...twice.

What in the hell am I doing? I wouldn't know what to do if he called my bluff. Chastity backed into the elevator doors as they slid open with Justin closing the gap between them.

"Obviously you don't follow instruction well, Matthews. I told you to stay away from me, and I mean it." *At least until I can figure out what to do with you once I know more about why Daddy insisted on whatever it was he insisted on.*

Chastity pressed the lobby button and the elevator doors closed, offering no escape until they landed at the first floor. Leaning against the back wall, Chastity closed her eyes for a brief instant. All she needed to do was get to the lobby and out the front doors and she'd be in the clear.

Her body lurched as the elevator came to a stop. Opening her eyes, she saw Justin's finger on the stop button. "What the hell are you doing, Matthews?"

He smiled, sweet and sexy. "Seeing if you can follow instruction or not."

Chapter 4

In three steps, Justin stood less than a foot from Chastity. Her sexual arousal filled his senses. An unusual mix of musk and wood with a touch of lavender, the aroma sweet and heady, sent his blood flow pounding to the tip of his cock.

The small of her throat pulsed, begging for him to kiss her there. "I, ah, don't know what you're getting at, Matthews. But you do need to get this elevator moving, or I'll...," she said, swallowing and wetting her dry lips.

If he could lick the dryness from her mouth, she'd never thirst for anything more in her life.

"You'll do nothing but listen to my instructions, Chastity." Reaching out, he lightly ran his fingers over her right nipple. He growled softly, feeling the clip where he'd left it, attached to her scrumptious bud.

"Don't," she mewed, thrusting her breast into his fingertips despite her weak protest.

"Mmmm, I think it's quite the opposite, Ms. Langford." He pressed firmly against the nipple, reveling at the moan escaping from his mate. His cock pushed against his zipper, throbbing to be free of its imprisonment.

She held onto the elevator railings, inviting him to explore more of her. And he would, as soon as he got her lessons over with for the day.

Justin flicked the jeweled clip through the material covering it, causing her to quiver against him. "Do you know what this represents, Chastity? It shows who you belong to for all time. Only in death will it ever be removed."

"God, Justin, what are you doing to me?" Her words, no more than a whispery breath, excited him more than if she'd grabbed his groin outright.

"Nothing more than your father instructed, Chastity." He firmly pressed his thigh just above her mound. She sighed hotly against him then spread her legs to allow him full access, sending his manhood into wild fits of thumping.

She stiffened slightly, and he ground against her. She jutted against his balls in response to his moving in a slow circle just below her belly.

"What does my father have to do with you seducing me?" She wetted her lips and held his gaze. There were flames of passion burning in her yellow ember eyes, and he moaned with his own heated desire.

"Why everything, Chastity," he responded, licking the pulsing point of her long, delicate neck.

Justin firmly grabbed her hand as she moved it from the railing. "Not until I give you permission, Chastity. Then and only then can you move your arms." Unbuttoning the neckline of her dress until her breasts were exposed, Justin kissed the tip of her cleavage, sending goose bumps dancing upon her skin. Triumph sailed through him as she pressed into him, urging his exploration to go further. It would take all his human instincts not to, for his animal impulses neared the edge of no return.

"You are delicious, Chastity." He gave her cleavage a final lick, savoring the salty taste of her body on his tongue. Reaching for the elevator stop button, he sent the machine on its interrupted journey. "Too much sweetness at one time will spoil one's appetite."

***

The elevator lurched, causing Chastity to steady her shaking legs. If this was what it was like to be made love to, she wanted more of it, and she wanted it now. He was not going to leave her wanting again.

"If you think for one minute we're done here, you are sadly mistaken, Matthews." She slammed the button, bringing the elevator to a jolting stop.

"*Think* is the wrong word, Chastity. More like we are certainly done, and that's all there is to it." Justin pushed the lobby button, thrusting the elevator into motion.

"I don't think so." Chastity drew in a breath to steel her doubts as she crossed the small expanse and pushed Justin against the wall. "Daddy always told us to finish what we've started, and I'm about to actually do as Daddy says for once."

Give me strength and don't chicken out now, Chas. She straddled him, wrapping her legs around his hips. The hard length of his rod bumped against her wet panties, sending her clit twitching.

He moved them around until her back was against the wall, and he ground against her clit.

"Yes. Ohhhh, Justin."

He pinched her nipples hard, giving each a quick twist. The sensation as the clip tightened around her nipple aroused her more than she could have imagined. Clinging to his shoulders, she nipped at his ear, feeling a rush of power soar through her.

"Is this what you want Chastity? You want to be fucked in an elevator by a man you despise?" He ground harder into her pussy, and she hugged herself closer to him.

"Yes, Justin. I want you inside me before I cum." She reached down in an attempt to unzip his pants when the elevator doors slid open.

"Shit, Chas. At least it's not that damn vibrator."

Chastity stiffened and could have died at the sight of her father standing in the doorway.

***

"Hello, Charles." Justin looked over his shoulder, releasing some of the pressure against Chastity as her legs slipped from around his hips.

"Justin," Charles nodded, a wicked smile crossing his face.

Chastity straightened her dress then pushed away from Justin. For having caught one of his daughters in a compromising situation, her father was awfully calm. She imagined most fathers would have killed the guy trying to seduce their daughter in a public elevator.

"Daddy, I, ah..." Her brain couldn't come up with an explanation, let alone her mouth form the words. What would she say anyway? That she was the one who initiated this particular moment? That she wanted to lose her virginity in the company elevator to a man she both desired and despised?

"I don't want to know, Chas." Charles laughed softly at her embarrassment. "Justin, are you quite through here?"

Justin faced her, looking her over as if he was anything but finished. "For the moment," he said, lust and desire flickering in his eyes.

"Good. We've got some business to discuss." Charles turned from them, and then after a step, paused. "I'll meet you in my office in, oh say, ten minutes."

"Ten minutes, Charles." Justin straightened his pants, tucking in the shirt she'd begun to pull from its neat package. "Well, Chastity, that's it for tonight. I'll see you in the morning."

Chastity gave him a shove and then buttoned her dress. "Wait a second! If you think for one cotton pickin' minute that I do this sort of thing all the time, you're crazy, Matthews." The lingering heat of his lips singed her skin; the heat traveling through her fingers as they slid the round buttons into their holes. She'd love nothing more than to do this all the time, especially with a man as skilled as Justin appeared to be.

"Chastity, my love, I've no doubt that you are about as experienced with physical love as Barbie and Ken are." Justin gave her nipple a quick flick of a finger then captured her mouth fully with his. He tasted like clover, sweet and powerful.

"But you will be, Ms. Langford. You will be," he stated, turning to follow in her father's footsteps.

Chastity heard her father's laughter as he walked through the lobby and past the company's information desk. Was it seeing his oldest daughter's legs wrapped around a man, or the look of surprise on their faces when the elevator doors opened that her father found so amusing?

She may never know for sure, but she'd bet Justin Matthews was about to be released of his duties at Langford and Langford.

Chapter 5

"Can I presume from what I witnessed that my daughter's taking to your instructions?" Charles commented without looking up from his laptop.

"You could say that," Justin laughed, sitting in the cranberry-colored leather wing-backed chair opposite Charles. "She's...quite receptive."

Charles pushed the laptop over to Justin, pointing to an email he'd been reading. "Good, from what Lash says, there's confirmation Lucas is being held by his sire, Rowan Angus, in the Beta encampment."

"Shit!" Justin shook his head. The worst fear of Charles and the Elite wolfen clan was now a reality. An offspring of one of their own, Lucas, had disappeared without a trace years ago. To keep peace, the clan was lead to believe he'd run away. Charles and the other leaders felt it would be in the clan's best interest not to know the truth about the attack and covered up the true reason for Justin's aunt's death. "What kind of condition is he in?"

Justin had known sooner or later this day

would come, as it had in Remington. As one of the last survivors of the Sinclair clan, it was the reason he'd been sent to the United States and the Langford clan. He'd quickly come to understand the importance of not letting the Betas know who he was. His true identity would complicate things for the Elites.

"I can't really tell. Lash indicates his informant says Lucas is being held on display like a prized animal. He's kept in a cage behind plexiglass in less than ideal conditions. I wonder what Rowan has in mind." Charles sat back in his chair, tapping his pen on the desk.

"I'm sure it's the usual, tearing us down and gaining power. Justin, I fear their leaders are stirring the Beta rank and file for the bonding night. The night of the blue moon is when they can take us at our weakest moment...during the breeding and bonding ritual. If they can turn Lucas against us and harness his growing powers now that he's reached his full potential, they just might stand a chance of destroying us."

"You know that's when they took our village, and it wasn't a pretty sight. We've got to take care of this well before then, which doesn't really leave us much time, does it?" Fear and determination pushed blood rushing to Justin's head. The thought of a fight avenging his family as intoxicating as the breeding ritual...both would mean the clan's survival. It would be a bloody and death-filled battle of survival for both clans. "If we can avoid the attack during this season of the blue moon, it would give us more time to gather our forces before the next ceremonial season."

"We may not have the luxury of that much time. Lash is the chosen one for Charity. Without him, I'm afraid Chari may live her life mate-less, and I can't have any of my girls living an empty life. And you know he'll go to any lengths to rescue his half-brother, up to and including risking his own neck."

"Then we'll have to back him, that's all there is to it." Justin pushed himself out of the chair. Lash's informant would have to come up with more than the email revealed. The Elite forces needed to know when the Beta's weakest moment occurred on a daily basis. Then they'd attack and take back Lucas, regardless that he may be brainwashed and confused about where he truly belonged.

"We've got our work cut out for us." Justin looked out over the dark expanse of the Jefferson River. Just on the other side of its banks, the Beta clan's encampment laid hidden deep within the dense Brey Forest. "If we don't get to them, first life, as the Elites know it, will all but vanish. The men will be subject to the breeding farms, and our women will be raped and treated like nothing more than sex slaves until the Betas tire of them."

"As an Alpha, Lucas's senses will be running, ramped between his human instincts and his wolf ones. Much like a half-breed in the human society, he wouldn't be sure where he belonged. Or which clan wants him for more than just a prized possession."

Charles had promised his best friend,

Justin's Uncle Krayton, on his deathbed, just weeks after Lucas' abduction, that they'd bring him home where he belonged. It was the reason why Charles had wandered into the streets so late at night.

Justin had failed to report to the Elite clan upon his arrival, and in doing so, a group of Elite warriors, under the direction of Uncle Krayton, wandered out to find him. His uncle eventually died from fatal injuries he'd sustained from a pack of Beta males. If Justin hadn't been in the alley that night, Charles would have died at the hands of a Beta group looking for him as well. It hadn't taken long for word to spread that a Sinclair descendant had arrived and had escaped capture before the good, bad, and the ugly had come looking for him.

***

The news about Lucas couldn't have come at a worse time. How in the hell was Justin going to balance Chastity's sexual instructions with that of rescuing a clan member, let alone keep his true identity hidden? A pure black wolfen was nearly as rare as a red, and the Betas knew their history well, despite their lowly existence. With the ritual less than a month away, he'd have to work fast on all accounts.

Uncle Krayton loved Lucas as much as he did Lash. Even as Aunt Madeline lay dying after the Beta clan's attack and Lucas' kidnapping, his uncle vowed to bring their son home to her. He'd promised her as much as she'd taken her last breath from the fatal injuries she'd suffered in the raid.

Lucas was a half-breed, a product of a rape during a Beta raid into an Elite encampment years ago. He'd had the good fortune of being accepted by his mother and her husband until he'd been captured during a deadly raid to his parents' home. As a fifteen-year-old Alpha, who was neither mostly wolf nor human, it hadn't been an easy fit for him. Justin's aunt and uncle did their best to nurture his strengths, easing the boy's growing confusion about who he was despite snobbery by others in the Elite clan. Even Lash bared his teeth on more than one occasion at anyone who caused his half-brother any harm, or even hinted at hurting him in any way.

With Krayton's death, Charles promised to help watch over Lash. He knew Lash's vow for revenge involved more than just the death of his parents. Lucas was a special Alpha, and Lash had felt it from the beginning. He'd confided in Justin more than once that Lucas was meant for far greater things than any of them could ever begin to imagine.

The question was whether or not Lucas would live long enough for Lash's prophecy to come true. Justin's plan was to have Lash's informant return from the forest with the Beta encampment's daily schedule. This would be the only semblance of order his raiding forces would be able to use in the rescue attempt.

The Betas were the lowest form of wolfen in the Midwest. They raped and planted their seed into any Elite she-wolf they could find. Once the babe came into the world and grew to the point where their powers began to emerge, the Beta warriors moved in to take claim of what they believed to be their property, killing the she-wolf before they left.

Justin couldn't be one hundred percent certain why they did what they did. He couldn't dismiss the rumors of a breeding farm in order to bring the Elite bloodlines into their society. Not much sickened him, but this rumor certainly gave his insides a twirl at the mere mention of the process. His sisters and mother had become victims of such a farm, until one night they'd hung themselves, ending their ordeal before he could rescue them.

Closing his eyes, the image of Chastity strung up and bred to like a dog invaded his mind. Knowing the Betas would do anything to get their hands on a princess, the very thought sent a wave of fear through his veins.

***

Chastity lurked just outside the doorway to her father's office. Her heart heavy, believing her father and Justin could be discussing the embarrassing situation in the elevator. She considered possible explanations to come up with to save Justin's job, but none of them rang true, even to her. After all, what does a daughter say to her father when he's just caught her in a very intimate situation?

"What do you propose then, Charles?" Justin stood looking out into the black of the night. When he turned, the moonlight played off his face, heightening the concern etching its way into his soul. Chastity wished she could kiss each line until they all disappeared from his handsome face. If she hadn't felt like she had to have the upper hand, none of this would be happening.

"I've been thinking about that and..."

Shit! They were already talking about proposals. The image of a shotgun wedding twisting her stomach, Chastity jumped away from the door, her heart racing like a rabbit caught with nowhere to run.

"You might as well come in, Chastity." Her father's irritated voice filtered through the slight opening of the door.

Damn it. She never was very good at being sneaky. Chastity took a deep breath to calm her quaking legs then stepped into her father's office. "Daddy, I, I..."

Charles stood, shaking his head. "It doesn't matter, Chas." He opened his arms and pulled her into them. How long had it been since her father held her this close? She couldn't remember, and right now, it didn't matter. He was her father and she was his little girl once again. His warmth and security enveloped her, chasing away her fears. She smiled, relieved that some things didn't change with age.

"We'll continue this meeting in the morning, Justin," he said, kissing her gently on her forehead. "Good night."

He stepped away, leaving her with the longing to be on his knee, riding that galloping pony as she did when she was three years old. Only this was far more serious than playing a child's game of giddy-up. Someone could be dismissed from their position because she couldn't control her sexual urges.

Chastity smelled Justin moments before he took her in his arms. The instant she felt his groin against her bottom, tidal waves surged through her. Her clit pulsed with horniness to feel him rub her mound again.

"It's been a long day, Chastity."

He lifted her off the floor and then cradled her in his arms. Her eyes met his and she knew in that one single moment she wanted him to make love to her.

Snuggling closer against him, Chastity wrapped her arms around his neck, capturing his mouth with her own. Her heart beat rapidly as he surrendered himself to her.

He tasted liked a good shot of whiskey...hot...salty...intoxicating. The first flavor burned going down and then lured you back for more. She drank him into her soul, wanting him more than life itself.

Chapter 6

Her heart pounded against his chest. Was her heavy breathing from fear of him or from being in his arms, which excited her? There was only one way to find out. "My sweet, Chastity," he whispered, nibbling on the edge of her ear. "One trip in an elevator, and you've become putty in my arms." Her lust-clouded eyes captured him, sending his rod throbbing in time with her heartbeat. He slipped his fingers into her, manipulating her pulsing clit. She was hot, wet, and ready for him, but he'd make her wait until he was ready to take her on his terms. Pressing her harder against the wall, he slipped another finger into her velvet folds. She moaned hotly and thrust her hips into his hand. His cock sprang into action...

Beep.

Justin squinted against the morning sun shining through the window. The sound of his answering machine became louder as he came up from the depths of sleep.

Beep.

Panic raced through him as he reached out next to him, praying that he'd indeed spent the night alone. The relief flooding him at the realization that he'd only been dreaming of seducing Chastity in the elevator did little to ease the ache in his crotch.

When in the hell had the phone rung? His acute hearing should have picked it up before the caller could leave a message. He'd been full of thoughts of planning Lucas' rescue and images of seducing Chastity, everything else escaped his otherwise sharp instincts. He couldn't let anything or anyone cloud his senses again. It was far too dangerous.

Beep.

"All right, damn it." Justin threw a pillow across the room at the machine, knocking it to the floor.

Tossing off the sheet, Justin got out of bed and stalked naked across the room. His cock stood straight and hard; begging for release. Once he made it to the bathroom, he wouldn't have to be concerned with a dream of fucking Chastity. That fantasy would be a distant memory, along with anything else his body wanted to be relieved of in the morning light.

Making his way across the room, Justin bent to pick up the annoying answering machine from the floor, pressing the message button as he set it back onto the table.

"Justin," Chastity's voice, soft and full of remorse, stopped him in his tracks. "I'm really sorry. I had no idea Daddy was still in the building. I...ah...well. Damn it, you must know you're not to blame for what happened tonight."

So, she thought an apology was in order. Justin smiled at the prospect of Chastity Langford offering him a sultry apology. *Will wonders never cease? I've brought a princess to her knees begging for forgiveness.*

"Anyway, it's late. I'm not sure what Daddy said to you. I'm so sorry Justin, whatever Daddy is making you do, if it has anything to do with me you, should forget about it. I'm not ready for something...permanent with a man I'm not in love with."

Justin laughed out loud. If she really knew what the future held for her, she'd be fit to be tied instead of so apologetic. Only he wasn't about to let her find out. No, she'd fall in love with him as much as he was with her. As much as he'd been since the first day he walked into Langford and Langford.

***

"Daddy?"

Chastity knocked on the door, pushing it open slightly. Her father's office held the silence from last night...full of secrets yet to be told. The air hung heavy with what she could only describe as deception, fear, and the unknown. She'd never noticed it before in his office, but then she hadn't noticed a lot of things before her sexual awareness. It felt like she was waking from a long winter's nap these days to a world changed, yet the same.

Disappointed her father had not yet come in the office, she decided to sit and wait for his usual arrival at six. Alone in the office, she cased the room, really looking at it.

Compared to the other offices in the company, her father's resembled that of an aristocratic library. Dark, rich, and definitely masculine, the room housed large leather chairs of hunter green and burgundy. Regardless of its rich elegance, Chastity much preferred the feminine tones of rose and mauve to greet her each morning.

The large watercolor painting on the wall behind her father's desk drew her attention. She must have seen the artwork a thousand times but never really took notice of it before now. It was beautiful and soothing to her senses. The muted strokes feathery—soft and alluring.

The blue hues mixed with the dark grays and blacks heightened her senses. The full moon set high in the sky held a hint of blue to it. The moon's rays shone down on an animal sitting in a grassy meadow. Not sure of whether it was dog-like or maybe even a bear cub, she got up for a closer look.

The painting drew her in. The peacefulness of the landscape enveloped her soul, warming the unexpected excitement building inside her. The pale blue tones of the moonlight washed over a black wolf sitting in the meadow surrounded by the tall grasses.

Chastity ran her fingers over the painted light as it washed over the wolf. A surge thrust through her as her fingers came to rest on the back of the wolf. Calmness in the mere act sent her juices flowing.

She moved even closer to the painting, becoming immersed until she felt every blade of the cool grass. She could feel the wolf's fur upon her skin, the smell both manly and wild. The sense of terror at touching the untamed animal absent.

For a brief moment, she felt the wolf's power take her in. Felt its eyes upon her as if she were there for him and no other. Her clit throbbed in response, wanting to be touched.

Running her fingertips over the deep green grasses, her breath hitched in her throat. In the grass lay a naked, strawberry blond-haired woman with the black wolf sitting between her legs and its paws upon her shoulders. Both the woman and wolf seemed to come to life, giving Chastity a sense of belonging.

***

Justin stood in the doorway watching Chastity become one with the painting. If she allowed herself to be drawn in any further, she'd be lost to them all. Carefully, so as not to startle her, he came up behind her. The scent of her sex was already strong and wild, like that of the she-wolf in human form lying in the tall grasses of the painting.

The piece of artwork symbolized everything the wolfen clan had become. It represented both their future and their past; humans with the heart of the wolf and wolves with the body of a human. When the two became one, magic occurred, but only during the mating ritual on the night of the blue moon.

He ran his fingertips lightly along her arms until his hands covered her delicate ones. The growth of need between his legs reminded him of the power she had over him. His cock needed her wrapped around him; to have her open up and pull him deep inside her body. He could feel her juices cover him like the coating on a chocolate-covered cherry.

He pulled her close to him, her ass bumping against his throbbing crotch. If only the night of passage were now and not weeks away, he could end the pain in his groin.

"I knew you'd be here," he whispered in her ear then backed away as she came out of her trance-like state.

She turned to look at him. Her yellow-green eyes reflecting the she-wolf passion growing inside of her. Her time drew nearer. He had to keep her close to him from here on in. The first time her wolfen-self took hold would be painful, much like a virgin losing her cherry. Quick sharpness followed by pleasure meant only for the male wolfen claiming her.

"Justin?" His name a mere whisper of breath off her lips. If she knew what was in store for her, for them, she might not want the answers to so many questions in her eyes.

He placed himself between her and the painting. Taking her hands in his own, he feather kissed the center of her palms. A shiver passed through her, onto his tongue, causing him to break the connection. It was getting too close for such games for him to take any chances; instead, he guided her around to the front of the desk.

"Beautiful, isn't it? The artist caught the very essence of the Night of the Blue Moon." He pulled her further from the watercolor, hoping the distance enough to allow a clean break from its allure.

Justin backed her into one of her father's burgundy wing-backed chairs until she sat snuggly in the leather. She peeked around his shoulder, pulling her hand from his. The disconnection left an unsatisfied need in his heart. He was head over heels and no one, not even rescuing Lucas, would stand in his way of making her his own. No other female, human or wolfen, would be able to satisfy the ache in his body.

Justin reached out and pulled open the window blinds, allowing the morning sun to fill the room with light. As the rays filtered through the window, they fell upon the painting, washing away the sexual magnetism that had captured Chastity. If it wasn't for the coming of the blue moon, she probably would have gone on without giving the canvas a second thought. Her heightened sexual awareness made her vulnerable to its magic; and for an untried wolfen, that only spelled disaster.

Chapter 7

"What the hell are the two of you doing in my office?"

Charles Langford stood with his arms crossed, waiting for an answer. Chastity knew he'd want one now, and the sooner the better. If her father had one fault, it was a lack of patience. Especially when he found unwanted bodies in his office before the sun had fully risen in the eastern sky.

Reluctantly, Chastity left the warmth and security of the chair. If she were going to confront her father about Justin, she wanted to do it standing and a little closer to being on equal ground with her father. Remaining seated in the chair would only put her in a position of vulnerability, and with her father, that could be a fatal mistake if she were to keep her nerve.

As a child, she'd seen him take out men with a mere look, and it was a fate she didn't want to experience...no matter how much she wanted something. She took a deep breath to slow the blood rushing to take leave of her head.

"I was hoping to talk with you, Daddy," She glanced back at Justin and clutched her arms across her breasts. He still stood near the windows, an amused look on his face. *Son-of-a-* .... "Alone!"

She turned from him and steeled herself for the storm she was sure would occur soon enough. Her father wasn't the type of parent who did well in the father-daughter talk area, unless it was business oriented. Then there was no stopping him from giving his opinion and seriously listening to what she, or her sisters, had to say. If it wasn't for her mother, they wouldn't even know about the things that happen as little girls grow into full grown women.

"What could you possibly have to say to me that couldn't wait, Chastity?" Charles pulled out his chair and sat, motioning for Chastity and Justin to do the same.

Holy shit. I can't do this in front of Justin. She drew in a deep breath and exhaled slowly, counting to five. "Daddy, I'd really rather not..."

She may be a softy where her father was concerned, but that didn't mean she'd have to show her weaknesses in front of Justin. What would he think, seeing her cower to her father and ask him to forgive Justin for what took place in the elevator? She didn't think he was the type of man who wanted, or needed, a woman to champion him...no matter what the reason.

Charles drew in a heavy breath, sending a shiver of warning through her. The shit was about to hit the fan if she was forced to beg for Justin's position in the company to be retained.

As much as she hated to admit it, he had a way with people she didn't. Langford and Langford needed him to get the best of the best; she'd use that reasoning with her father.

"Chastity Lynne Langford," he spat, shoving himself from the desk. "I've had just about enough of your childishness. You're a grown woman, damn it. It's about time you acted like one. You and your sisters are trying my patience with your strange sexual practices you think no one knows about."

She'd never seen her father this angry, or frustrated before. His eyes grew dark with irritation as he leaned over the desk. There had to be something more going on. Finding his eldest daughter humping his star pupil wouldn't set him off like this, would it?

"What's going on?" Chastity looked from her father's glazed-over face to Justin. If she could wipe the smile off Justin Matthew's face, she'd reach out and do it. But she wasn't Stretch Armstrong and had no aspirations of feeling his skin upon hers ever again.

Men! They're all the same and make no sense at all.

"Damn it, daughter! I don't want to hear about your frustrations or fantasies or how you were only trying to sexually relieve yourself like some wild bitch in heat." Her father stood inches from her, his eyes a fiery shade she'd never seen before. It was as if he were possessed by some demon. "Now get the hell out of my office."

She stood, fighting through the tears threatening to overtake her. "Up yours, Mr.

Langford." If she broke down here, she'd look like nothing but a silly, weepy female to both Justin and her father. She'd go to Hell before she'd let either of them know that her heart was breaking into a million pieces.

***

Fucking A! What the hell was that about? "Christ, Charles. Did you have to be so blunt about it? I thought you were going to morph right then." Justin watched Chastity walk through the office door with as much dignity as she could. If she'd been a man, he was sure she would have punched her father in the nose, if not knocked him out. She'd be a hellcat the more she stewed on her father's comments, and he'd be the one left to deal with her. Damn Charles, the clan, and that miserable blue moon.

"It was the only way I could guarantee she'd leave. We've got to talk about rescuing Lucas before the blue moon, or this clan will be in grave danger of becoming extinct."

Charles once again sat behind his desk, mulling over some papers he'd scattered across the top of it. Getting involved with this rescue attempt was the last thing Justin had on his mind. He had a red-haired princess to get ready for the binding ceremony in a few weeks.

"I presume you've got a plan, Charles." Justin sat in the chair vacated by Chastity, her sweet, lavender scent lingered, raising his sexual awareness of her. Damn but the she-wolf had a way of getting to him.

Charles nervously shifted in his chair, a sign

that he wasn't sure of whatever lay in front of him. His furrowed brow meant he'd been mulling things over in his head. "All reports indicate that they've been using Lucas as a breeding wolf. His Beta half-brother, Kill, wants to see him dead, so my guess is when we attack, Kill will send his sentries to kill Lucas."

"Let me guess, Lash wants to get him out of his prison hold *before* they even know our army's outside their encampment." Justin got up, looking out the window into the morning sun just above the tree tops along the lakeshore. Somewhere in that forest, their worst enemy lay in wait.

"Exactly."

Justin turned, seeing for the first time age beginning to play its webbed lines around the clan leader's eyes. "Someone will need to stay here to protect the clan. It could be a ploy to get us away from the safety of the city so they can attack and take prisoners."

Charles' chest heaved with a great sigh. "And take my daughters for their breeding program."

Cold fear soared through Justin's heart. If the Betas got their grimy paws on the Langford girls, it would be a fate worse than death. "What does Lash's source say?"

"See for yourself," Charles said, handing him an email printed out. "It's not pretty by any stretch of the imagination, which they lack plenty of."

Justin scanned the paper quickly. Blue moon. Princesses. Breed. If those words meant what he thought they did, the Elites were in grave danger. None more so than the Langford sisters.

"I'm counting on you, Justin. One day, I'll be too weak to guide the clan. The young wolves won't want to follow an old silver beard, but will a pure black." Charles was only inches behind Justin as he studied the paper. "The prophecy of the painting must come true. The black wolf and the red-haired human, you and Chastity, during the night of the blue moon, must revitalize the clan for the future."

The sun continued its climb into the sky, waking a new day for all who cared to live.

"You are the chosen ones, Justin."

The words, a mere whisper in the air, reverberated in Justin's mind and heart. They were the same words his family recited to him throughout his childhood, that one day he'd take his rightful place in the clan with a red-haired princess. His wolf's mind became sharper while his human heart stronger with desire. Battlement and the night of claiming his she-wolf became one in both those sacred places, and Justin knew what he must do.

Chapter 8

Chastity slammed her office door, turning the lock. If her father thought for one minute that he'd be able to worm his way into making an apology, he was sadly mistaken. His words had cut deep and the wound had already begun to fester.

"Maybe the next time, he'll find me and Justin screwing, then what would he call it?" She opened her office blinds and looked out over the Jefferson River. The rays of the morning sun were just making their way through the trees of the Brey Forest, casting glistening figures of light off the calm water.

The ever-changing shimmer played with her imagination. The rays took on the shape of a wolf-like creature standing on its hind legs. Its face took human form, showing anger mixed with fear. There looked to be shackles around its ankles, with a woman-like creature on her hands and knees in front of him. Her back slanted down, her ass moved closer to the wolf's shaft.

The creature struggled against the restraints

until the woman-like figure's ass swallowed his rod. The wolf creature began pumping the woman wildly, the chains swaying with each movement.

Chastity felt her own channel become wet with moisture, and her clit throbbed with a need she'd never felt before. She placed her hand over her mound and began rubbing it in a circle, until her fingers were between her lips. Even through her clothing she felt her juices penetrating her slacks. Her right nipple hardened into the clip still attached to it. Her hips moved with the motion of the shimmering vision...

SNAP! Darkness shut out the light of the sun. She turned to find the blurry form of Justin with the wooden blind's wand in his hand.

"Chastity?"

His voice sounded far off, in the distance. Her fingers wouldn't stop moving, she was so close to coming. She needed the shimmering vision, just one more second, and she would have screamed with release.

"Chastity, tell me what you've seen." Justin's voice was closer now, pulling her out of her trance. But she didn't want to go, not yet. Not until she'd cum all over in her pants, she needed to let it go.

"Fuck me, Justin." She grabbed his hand, held it to her pussy and rubbed against it. Her vision still blurred, his handsome face turned to that of the black wolf in the painting. Powerful and full of passion, she wanted to feel what the creatures in her vision felt.

"Christ, not like this."

Chastity turned and leaned over so her ass bumped against his groin. Feeling his hardness between her cheeks, she pushed herself into him until she felt her juices begin to flow hotter. She didn't know what was happening except that she was on the verge of a sexual release she'd only read about.

***

"I need you to..."

Her words echoed in Justin's ear, tempting him to rip the slacks from her body and bury himself deep into her. His cock, harder than it had ever been, seemed to grow each time she ground her ass against it.

"Chastity," he growled, feeling the wolfen begin to emerge.

He'd have to rely on his human strength to take control before his wolf instincts came out. Grabbing her ass, he placed his hand over her cunt mound. His fingers found her clit and began stroking until he felt her quiver and collapse in his arms.

It wasn't much, but it was all she'd get from him...this time.

"Chastity, can you hear me?" He nuzzled her ear, the smell of her sex filling his nostrils.

"Mmmmm."

Scooping her into his arms, Justin gently set her down on the Victorian loveseat in her office. If she only knew what would have happened to her if he hadn't let himself into her office. The magic of the mating season was coming on too strong, even the sunlight rays were drawing her into the web.

"Justin?"

He drew in a quick breath to steady his mind and his shaking body. "Are you okay?"

Chastity sat up slowly, looking a little dazed. "I-I think so. What happened?"

He sat beside her, taking her hand in his. "Tell me what you saw, Chastity."

How much could he tell her without blowing her mind? How much would she think was fabricated and what was truth? Twice in one day she'd seen the vision of the black wolf and a red-haired woman...their destiny.

"I was looking out over the water when I imagined seeing a man, but more like a wolf..." she explained, her voice shaking and uncertain if it had only been her imagination fueled by the painting in her father's office. "And a woman bent over in front... What's happening to me, Justin?"

"There's something you need to know." Moisture beaded upon his upper lip, he was about to spill the beans before the can was even open. Charles would have his head, but he didn't care. He loved this woman and couldn't stand to see her go through this transition any more.

"Langford and Langford is in trouble. There's a group of...investors who have been after it for years, and the time is drawing that they may make a move to take it over." Justin walked over to the blinds and pulled them open. The sun, now high in the sky, no longer posed a threat to his mate.

"That's why Daddy's so uptight then." She

moved across the room to join him.

"You might say that." Her sexual scent still strong, Justin moved away, not trusting himself. "There's a bit more to it than a takeover of the company." Standing in front of the ornate oval mirror surrounded by silk lavender plants, Justin glanced at his image. *Shit! Not yet...it's too soon for this to be happening.*

Fear soared through him; the blue star sapphire to match Chastity's grew more vivid to where she'd be able to see it in a matter of minutes. He had to see if it was happening to her too. If her mating symbol was emerging, they'd not be able to wait for the night of the blue moon, they'd have to mate now before the enemy got any closer.

***

Chastity stood, feeling totally helpless. There was a possible takeover of the company and her father hadn't come to her and her sisters to help him? Why wouldn't he? Didn't he believe they were strong enough to ward off these enemies? After all, an attempted stock takeover wasn't anything new in the business world. Charity possessed the knowledge to stop any such challenge.

"Chastity," Justin called out to her, his voice gruff and strange to her. There was something more going on.

God no! "Daddy. He's not dying is he?" She cried out, reaching for Justin's arm. If anyone would know, it would be Justin. Her father had been keeping Justin close to him these past years, but closer than any of the other people in the company the last few weeks. Even his own daughters had been kept at arms' length.

Not that they'd given it a second thought. They'd been too full of their newly found sexual urges to pay attention to what was happening in the company they'd been raised to take over one day.

"No, he's not." Justin turned from the mirror, a strange look on his face.

"Justin," she began, walking slowly over to him. "What's that on your face?" How in the hell had he gotten a bruise between his eyes? Had he and her father gotten into a fight after she'd left her father's office?

The bruise took form as Justin stepped toward her, and for the first time, she noticed a headache forming just between her eyebrows. The closer Justin got to her, the more intense the pain became. She'd never had migraines before, and this was more than just sinus.

She closed her eyes as Justin took her in his arms, kissing away the pain between her eyes. His lips were hot and soothing, easing away everything that hurt. Her father's harsh words, the need for sexual fulfillment, Justin's continued rejection of her...everything that caused her even the smallest bit of emotional emptiness.

His lips trailed down her neck, sending hot shivers through her body. His hand passed over the nipple still held by the clip he'd placed there hours ago. Her clit twitched with hardness when his finger flicked at the jewel.

"You're mine, Chastity, and no one else's," she heard him growl into her ear. He continued to manipulate the buttons on her blouse until her breasts were exposed. With a nip and a flick of his tongue, he had her writhing against him.

She pressed her hand against the zipper of his pants, feeling the bulge smoldering against her palm from the other side. He felt huge and grew larger as she rubbed her fingers up one side and down the other.

"Justin, please take me." She heard the words, not realizing what she begged from him.

She felt her slacks being ripped from her body. His fingers plunged into her, and she sunk closer against him.

She pulled the zipper of his pants down until his engorged cock sprung free. Wrapping her fingers around it, she moved her hand up and down the shaft. He growled softly in her ear, the sound giving her encouragement to continue.

"Is this what you want, Chastity?" His fingers continued to stroke first her clit then her channel as he spun her around. Her ass brushed up against his hardness and she gasped, waiting to see if he'd push against her.

"Justin, please take me." Each time she rotated her ass slightly against him, he shoved his fingers deeper into her. Spreading her stance wider, she wanted to feel him against more than her butt cheeks. As she did so, Justin pulled her forward with one of her nipples until she was on her hands and knees in front of him.

"Are you sure you want this mating, Chastity?" His knees spread her legs further apart until the tip of his cock played at the opening of her pussy. His fingers still manipulated her clit and she became hotter and wetter. She burned with desire to have him inside her.

"Yes!" she growled as he shoved his cock into her, and she wrenched at the sharp pain. He filled her pussy, stretching it with each stroke until the pain ceased and all that remained was the pleasure of feeling him inside her. He pumped her like the image she'd seen in the water; two wild animals fucking without a care if anyone saw them or not.

They were the black wolf and the red-haired woman in the light of the blue moon.

When she opened her eyes, she saw their reflection in the mirror. Between their brows was a matching blue star sapphire symbol, and they were fully clothed.

Chapter 9

Charles sat in his office waiting for Justin to report back to him after the mating had begun. Yes, he'd been hard on Chastity, maybe a little too hard. He'd done it for the girl's own good, at least that's what he kept telling himself over and over again for the past two hours.

"What the hell is taking so long?" He got up out of his chair and made his way to the vast bulletproof windows overlooking not only the Jefferson River and Brey Forest, but he also had a bird's eye view into his daughters' offices. The blinds to Chastity's office shut out his view.

He'd seen the faint she-wolfen look in Chastity's eye way too early, forcing their hands to move forward. The symbolic painting was not to become known to her for another seven days, when they'd had more time to prepare for the binding. But that was a mere technicality when it came to protecting his daughter. She needed someone to focus her growing need on, she needed Justin. Charles was sure Rowan Angus, the Beta leader and his mortal enemy, had found a way to move time forward.

The sun had begun its magic web of sinful allure over his daughter. First with showing her the painting, then reflecting off the river, its shimmering figures called out to her through the windows of her office. It was evident, as he watched her from his office windows. He'd guessed what was going on, and it scared the hell out of him. Luckily, he'd given Justin the right to claim her before the sun sat too high in the morning sky.

If he hadn't, Rowan's evil forces may have taken her, and they had enough to deal with before the blue moon rose and the ceremony began to allow that to happen. Lucas' life was in danger as well, the clan didn't need the complication of rescuing two members of their clan all in one night.

"Come on, Justin. How long can it take to mate with a woman anyway, even if she is my daughter?" Charles paced around the room, his nerves strung tighter, edgier than ever before. "Why would Rowan choose now to try to take claim to the clan? Why after all these years would he attempt to take what rightfully didn't belong to him?"

"Because the time's right, Charles, and you know it. With a direct Sinclair descendent amongst the Elite, the taking is all the sweeter, don't you think?"

Charles spun toward his opened office door to find Rowan standing in the doorway. Charles' hackles were up and his heart pounded...the enemy was in his camp. How had he gotten past their defenses? The Beta leader had never dared to step into their camp, let alone his office before. Danger was on the horizon sooner than any of them thought.

The prophecy of his daughters was well known and documented in the clan's history. It didn't take a genius to figure out they were the key to the survival of the Elites. With the arrival of Justin, Charles may have underestimated the Beta leader. Maybe Rowan had more brains then they'd given him credit for.

"What do you want, Rowan?" Charles took control of his body, maintaining his human form until he found out what the rogue wolf wanted. "You've violated the ancient peace treaty our perspective clans agreed to over a hundred years ago."

Rowan laughed, shaking his head. "Only the Elite Princesses could cause such a breach of contract, and of course there's the presence of Justin Sinclair," he said and then dematerialized into the air. "This may be your only warning, old friend. Heed it."

Charles quickly looked out the window over to Chastity's office. Relief flooded his body as he saw the open blinds, giving him the signal that their mating had ended. Cold enveloped him as he struggled to keep on his feet and from falling into the black hole waiting for him. He pitched forward; Rowan's snarling laughter following close behind the sound of his daughter's voice.

***

"What does my father have to do with this,

this mark you've put on my face?" Chastity pushed past Justin and then turned to face him. "What the hell is going on, Matthews?"

"I told you. It's a mating mark, something of a birth mark, and I didn't put it there. You've always had it." *I don't need this right now. I can smell a Beta wolf's been here.*

"That's plain old bullshit and you know it. No two people could possibly have the exact same mark in the exact same place, it's impossible." Chastity stood with her hand on her forehead, as if she could rub the symbol from her face. "Damn it, Justin! How and why did this appear? There's more to this than you're telling me and I demand to know the answers...NOW!"

"It wouldn't be any easier for you to understand if we were normal people, but we're not, Chastity. You can feel it in your soul, the changes that have been coming on stronger and stronger." Justin took her by the arms and physically moved her out of his way. Something was going on in Charles' office and he needed to get there quick. "Now, come on. We are expected in a meeting with your father and you know how he is if someone's late."

He turned from her, hoping her she-wolf senses would kick in, even though he knew deep in his heart it was too soon for her to take form. She didn't know or understand how to harness the power to turn from human to wolf and back again without hurting herself and those around her.

Chastity's growl brought a smile to his face as he walked quickly to the end of the hallway. If she'd only listen to herself, she'd realize what was going on. That she was changing; that the world as she knew it in her human mind was changing.

A low, snarling laughter reached his ears, raising the hair on the back of his neck. *Damn it, Rowan!*

"Justin! Get back here. I'm not done with you yet."

Sprinting down the hall, Justin felt his skin prickle and his bones elongate. He leapt into the air, black, coarse hair replacing his Armani suit. Landing on all fours, he loped down the hall, growling low. Charles was in trouble and he needed to protect the elder wolfen before Rowan had a chance to destroy him.

***

Holy shit! Fear gripped Chastity's soul and she reached out to the wall for support. *A wolf! Justin. Where's Justin?* Her heart pounded as she gasped for the air that quit circulating through her body. Her mind swirled in painful circles. She breathed in deeply, gaining control of her body until she felt steady on her feet.

"Justin!" Chastity ran down the hall in the path Justin had taken before the wolf appeared in his place.

A low warning growl reached her ears, stimulating her primal senses. Her father was in trouble; she didn't know how she knew, she just did. The dreadful snarling continued as she raced toward his office.

Chastity stood motionless in the doorway of

her father's office. Two wolves, one black as night and the other silver grey, crouched near her father's lifeless body like two carnivores about to fight over dinner.

"Daddy!" Her words nothing more than a snarl, she sprang forward to where her father laid sprawled out on the floor, putting herself between her father and the creatures in his office.

"Chastity?" His words sounded like a blast in her ears. She huddled closer, protecting Charles with her body. The wild animals in his office would have to kill her if they thought they were going to get to her father.

The rumble of a low growl came deep within her as she looked from one wolf to the other. The grey wolf backed away, as if it were unsure of her sudden presence in the room. It disappeared into the air followed by the word, "Princess."

"Chastity?"

Trembling, she jumped at the sound of Justin's voice next to her. She turned straight into the face of the black wolf, with the same sexy eyes as Justin.

Chapter 10

"Are you okay, Charles?" Justin stood. He hadn't meant for Chastity to see him in his wolfen form just yet. Charles being attacked left him with no other choice. If only he hadn't indulged himself so long in the luxury of Chastity's body and the feel of her wrapped around him, he may have prevented the attack from happening.

The wolfen eased from his body. Soon his human side would be fully emerged from the depth of darkness. It had been years since the wolf had come forth, not since his early teens during his coming out ceremony for the male Elites shortly after helping Charles fight off a rogue pack. It had been a time of uncertainty as well as jubilation for the pack, welcoming the young males into the fold. Being a bit older than most of the young males, Justin thought it was more of a way to celebrate Charles' life being spared more than anything.

Seated at his desk, Charles sat with his head resting against the back of his chair. "Thanks to you, I'm alive." He looked around the room then focused his attention on Justin. "Where's Chastity?"

Snapping his pants shut, Justin wasn't sure if Charles remembered his daughter being in the room protecting him from a couple of wolves or not. *Let's hope she believes it was all a dream. That she didn't see Rowan or me as werewolves.*

"I have no idea." He dared not look at the long-time clan leader and mentor. He was sure the lie would be seen in his face, and then he'd be forced to tell him exactly what happened. That his daughter had acted like a she-wolf protecting her young. She'd moved like a wolf, yet hadn't changed from her human form.

"She saw you, didn't she?" Charles' face fell with grief when Justin nodded. He knew she saw more than Charles realized. She'd witnessed Rowan dematerializing and the beginning of his own transformation from wolf to human. Her look of disbelief burned deep in Justin's heart; he wanted to spare Charles the knowledge of his daughter's fear and disgust.

"I'm at a loss, Justin. How in the hell did Rowan breach our defenses?" Charles went to stand up, only to sink back down in the chair. "Damn it!"

"I've no idea." Justin turned toward the window and looked over into Chastity's office. "She's not hurt, Charles. For that you can be thankful and a bit more relaxed."

"Time has sped up, Justin. If you didn't start the mating, she'll fall victim to the Betas...or worse."

Justin's cock swelled with the memory of

their mating. She fit perfectly around him, like a custom made glove...warm and snug. Chastity's willing aggressiveness may have put off any other man, but not Justin. No, he liked her going for what she wanted.

Looking out the window over to the Brey Forest on the shores of the Jefferson River, a sense of dread came over him. He knew all too well what was brewing in the trees, and he didn't like it one bit.

"It has begun, Charles." He flipped the blinds closed, shutting out the warning he sensed coming from the Beta encampment.

***

Chastity couldn't get far enough away from the nightmare she'd been made a part of. All she understood was she'd been hovering over her father's body, hoping to keep the pair of wolves from killing him. Instead, she'd witnessed the wolves turning from beast to man...more to the point, werewolf to man.

Werewolves were mythical beasts made up by some European town to ward unwanted people away. Such creatures just didn't exist in her sleepy little Wisconsin town; nor in her father's office building for that matter. They only existed in the minds of warped people with no life of their own.

Chastity sat on the edge of the river, trying to sort things out in her mind. If she'd gone to see her mother instead of running to her favorite childhood spot, she might have answers to some incredible questions. As a child, the calmness of the river and the warmth of the sun always seemed to chase away the chill of fear.

She couldn't find its solace today.

"You mustn't fear him."

Chastity didn't need to turn around to know where the words came from. Her mother's voice, clear and soft, came to her senses...even if she wasn't physically next to her. Smiling, memories of her mother always knowing when she needed her surfaced. And she never needed her more than right now.

"Mama, I don't fear him as a man...just what he turned into." Chastity played with a blade of grass, its sides distinctly different. One smooth and one a little rough against her fingers, much like Justin.

"Are the differences between that blade of grass and Justin so different?"

Chastity picked another and examined it a little closer. Without touching the plant, she'd never feel the difference. Was it the same with Justin? She knew it was.

Chastity put her head in her hands, hiding her face with shame. *"Justin's not real, Mama."* Taking a deep breath, she looked across the water for strength to tell her mother about Justin. *"I let him touch me in places only a husband should touch a woman."* A tear slipped down her cheek, landing on the green blade between her fingers.

"Then you've seen the mating mark that matches Justin's. Do you love him?"

She sighed deeply with relief. He hadn't lied to her after all. Feeling the smile fill her face with warmth, she closed her eyes. *"Yes, more than life. He's everything a woman like me could want."* Chastity let another tear fall, landing on top of the other. Her words were spoken with truth...a truth she hadn't realized until now.

"A woman like you, Chastity?"

"Mama, what am I going to do? I'm in love with and had sex with a man who turns into a werewolf."

Her mother's laughter warmed her soul. *"As have I, and I wouldn't trade the past thirty-five years for another life. The love your father and I have for each other has given us three beautiful daughters."*

Chastity's heart thundered in her head. *"Daddy's one too?"*

"He comes from one of the most powerful of wolfen societies. Your father's the Elite leader. But, I'm a human with unusual powers who couldn't resist the charms of a big, bad wolf. You and Charity are like your father, while Clarity takes after me."

"Do they know?"

"Not yet, but they will when the time's right for them...as it is for you. Go to your mate, Chastity, and embrace your destiny."

The warmth of her mother's presence grew faint, leaving Chastity with her own thoughts. She needed Justin as much as she loved him. If she were to survive and understand, she'd give all she could to bring children of her own into their world.

***

Justin strolled down the path leading to the river's edge. He had no idea what he would say to Chastity, other than telling her how much he needed her next to him. It took her seeing him morph to make him realize they weren't being fair to her, or her sisters. All the sneaking around and deception was no way to begin a relationship of any kind...let alone a love affair.

He was rounding the corner of the gardens when he heard it. An uncommon howl at mid-day on the private grounds of the company sent the blood rushing through his veins. He sniffed the air as he ran toward the river's edge.

Chastity! His upright position soon turned to that of an animal running on all fours. His mate was in trouble, and he'd tear the beast from limb to limb before allowing his human side to take form again.

A snow-colored wolf stood on the banks of the river, whining and prancing around the red wolf before being thrown through the air when it got too close. Approaching with caution, Justin paused as the wolf once again bounced off the shield of light surrounding the cowering red wolf.

Where in the hell is she? He slunk through the tall grasses, keeping to the river's edge. Coming up behind the red, he recognized the scent of his mate. Somehow Chastity had morphed into a wolf, but one with a force field around her.

Slowly he stepped into the vision of the silvery-white enemy, making himself known to him. The wolf's scent unfamiliar, he felt the beast was as fearful of Chastity as she was of him. *Maybe he's just a regular wolf following the scent of a she-wolf in heat. Then again, maybe not.*

He bared his teeth and took one step forward, sending the would-be foe back into the forest. The red she-wolf collapsed, and Justin watched with mixed emotions as the she-wolf transformed back into the woman he loved.

Morphing himself, Justin gathered her in his arms, wrapping her shivering body next to his. "Chastity?"

Her beautiful yellow-green eyes gleamed with tears. Pulling her closer, he kissed each tear from her eyes, cheeks, and anywhere else there happened to be one. Rocking her in his arms, he smoothed her long light reddish hair down over her back. Her nipples beaded against his chest. Their hearts pounded together, in sync with each other.

She clung to his shoulders, shaking with fear. "I was thinking of what it would be like, and the next thing I knew, my arms and legs were covered in fur and I was surrounded by a glowing bubble."

"Shhh, don't think about it now. We'll sort things out later, love." Justin continued rubbing her back and kissing her face. He wanted the fearless woman he'd made love to earlier in the day. He wanted to feel her aggressiveness envelope his body and take her as his own.

He pulled her closer, stood, and took a few cautious steps. Now that he had her in his arms, he'd never let her go. No matter what, this woman was his life...his sole reason for living.

"Not yet," she said, nipping him in his chest. For a quick moment, the scrape of her teeth sent his cock to attention. "Make love to me Justin...here and now."

A half moan half growl escaped him. It was too soon after morphing for them to make love; if they allowed this to happen before the blue moon binding ceremony, it could ruin their chances of being together forever. Somewhere, between human and wolfen, they were in a position that in time could produce an off-spring. A position he'd sworn an oath not to let happen until the night of the passage for their society.

"Justin," she whispered in his ear, her hand around his cock stroking it to hardness. "Please let me make you forever and always mine...as a woman."

"Chastity." His voice harsh and coarse sounded more like a snarl than words of love. She slipped from his embrace, pulling him down to the ground and straddled him. She held him in her hand then slowly slid down over the length of his shaft.

Her hot cunt grabbed him, sucking him deeper inside her. With each stroke she rode him, the harder he became. Unable to take any more, he flipped her over and onto her knees. He leaned over her and slid his fingers into her hot juices. Nipping at her shoulder, he pinched her clit before slamming into her from behind.

He slid deep inside her, filling her womb with his seed until their human side no longer existed.

Chapter 11

"She'll want answers now, Charles." Joanna stood next to her husband. She was the woman he'd mated and claimed as his own during their blue moon binding, even though his heart had been mending with the loss of another.

Charles looked at his woman, remembering how painful their mating had been for her. It wasn't every day a human woman accepted a werewolf as their mate, let alone their lover. But she had, knowing exactly what it would mean to them and their people. He hadn't known at the time how much she really loved him, or that she'd guide him along the path of finding love again.

"I'll be the one to tell her, Joanna. Chastity may be the most difficult of the three while Clarity will be the easiest. You understand Clarity's human nature better than I; you should be the one to explain to her about her sisters and their sudden fascination with sex." He turned and walked away from the window. The sky was already beginning to change, and if his calculations were correct, the blue moon would be less than twenty-four hours away.

Joanna's soft laugh filled his weary heart with warmth. "Clarity has known for some time, Charles. Sexual urges come very early in some humans, and our youngest is no exception. She understands she's different than her sisters, in more ways than one."

The shock of knowing his baby girl was most likely not a virgin swept through him. He'd always thought all three of his girls would come into their own in their thirties and mate with the best of their pack. To know Clarity could be human hadn't even occurred to him.

"She must be very much like her mother then." He pulled Joanna into his arms and nibbled on her ear. "And I wouldn't have it any other way. You'll have to find her a suitable—"

"Daddy!" Chastity's voice boomed into the room. "Oh, sorry..." she stopped short, the surprise of finding her parents in an embrace radiating across her face. It wasn't often they showed affection other than in their private bedroom.

"Hello, Chastity dear." Joanna hugged her daughter then took Justin in her arms. "Justin, thank you." She leaned in, giving his cheek a kiss and then left the room, a white light of protection surrounding her.

"Chastity, please close your mouth and sit down. It's very unbecoming of a...a woman of your age." Charles waited as first Chastity then Justin took a seat in front of him. He knew this day would come, and yet he was ill prepared for what he had to tell his daughter.

"What happened in here, Daddy? Who, what was that other wolf?"

All these years he'd pictured it as being as easy as explaining to her about the game of baseball. Faced with the task, he realized it was going to be anything but easy. The bases were different and they were reached for different reasons. Talking about sex would be hard enough, but how does one explain to their children that they aren't who, or what, they think they are? That in fact they are a creature movies are made of, but without all the lies and deception Hollywood throws in to sell tickets.

"I'm not sure where..."

"Daddy, please just tell me. No pretty wrapping. No French silk bow."

When did you grow up, little one? "Okay, if that's what you want. Our family has been living here for hundreds of years. Our ancestor, Remington Sinclair, came to the United States after being banished from his family for being...different."

Charles told Chastity and Justin how the Elites came to be and why they'd settled in the Brey Forest. He told them of how Remington had fallen in love with a local woman, married her, and started the Elite wolfen society.

"Our blood goes back to Remington Sinclair, the prince of a tiny European country. That makes you a princess."

"Princess? Princess of what? Werewolves?"

Charles searched his mind, trying to find the right way to start and not finding one. "Well, sort of. You are a princess and we are werewolves, but not in the sense you're thinking. The Elites aren't anything like Hollywood portrayed us. We don't wait for the full moon and then change into bloodthirsty beasts. If that were true, you'd have known about it by now."

It broke his heart to see tears stream down her face and knowing he couldn't do anything about it any longer. The daughter he'd been the closest to now turned to another for comfort. She turned to her mate.

***

A princess? How does he expect me to believe this? Chastity gripped Justin's hand with hers. Deep in her heart she knew what her father said was true, but her mind just couldn't fully accept it. Common sense told her people didn't turn into wolves, no matter how much proof they had to the contrary. Yet, she'd seen it for herself, right there in her father's office.

"You are the eldest of the Blue Moon Princesses. And highly prized by our people and our enemies who still live deep in the forest." Charles stood at the windows looking at the forest on the other side of the river. "They may make their move during the blue moon, when we'll be at our weakest."

Chastity sighed deeply, her blood rushing through her veins. Somewhere inside she knew her father spoke of the wolf that had attacked him earlier. Was the one she'd come across at the river's edge of that clan too?

"Then the wolf that was here, with Justin,

wanted to kill you?"

Her father nodded, his eyes full of anger and remorse as he walked back to his desk. "Rowan Angus once held a position in our society, despite his Beta blood. We'd grown up as childhood friends and secretly played along the river's edge. I didn't believe the elders' warnings and took him as my blood brother; it was the biggest mistake in my life."

"What happened, Daddy? If you were such good friends, what could have caused the split?"

"Ah...the love for another. I was promised a wolfen bride. It was someone Rowan loved and desired his entire life. When our union took place, he pledged to destroy not only the Elites, but also my family should I ever have one. Soon enough, his thirst for blood became strong and he'd planned his attack."

As if it could break any more, her heart fell into more shattered pieces when she saw the sorrow on her father's face. For the first time in her life, she thought her father was crying.

"But you survived, Daddy, as did Mama. What does he want now?"

"He wants you and your sisters, Chastity." Charles stepped away from his desk and pulled the cord hanging just behind him. As the curtain opened it revealed the painting Chastity had found so fascinating. "And Justin. Chastity, when we found you earlier, what did you see in this painting?"

Her body responded to the canvas as it had before. Liquid heat poured into her veins and her juices were beginning to drip. The deep need for sex grew within her and she looked to Justin, wishing they were alone.

"At first it was the soft colors, and then it was the rays of the moon. They're a pale blue and very soothing." Chastity stood and walked over to the painting, fingering the moon's rays. "It was as if I could feel the blades of the cool grasses all around me. I had a feeling of sensual pleasure when I found the naked red-haired woman with a black wolf between..." *Oh my god, Justin! It can't be Justin and me.*

"*This* is your destiny, Chastity." Charles pointed to the woman and the wolf. "You are the chosen one to bring our people back from the depths of despair. Along with Justin, who will protect you once the mating and bonding has begun, you'll be the first to bring the clan back to glory and respect. You and your sisters have special powers you've yet to find." Charles looked at her as if she were someone he should bow down to. "Justin's blood is of the oldest in our clan, and the most feared. Because of your hair, you are the most prized and sought after."

"A silver-white wolf was at the river's edge when I went to Chastity." Justin spoke from across the room. His voice distant yet very distinct in her mind. "There was a shield of white light around a red wolf, protecting her from his attacks."

"I didn't see a red wolf, Justin." Chastity shook her head, chasing away the image of her morphing limbs. "There was only the one that came out of the forest as if it were going to attack me. The next thing I remember is being in your arms."

Chastity felt her father's arms embrace her. He held her close, smoothing her long, strawberry-blonde hair down her back.

"You will see, Chastity. All you need to do is look into your heart and you will see her."

Charles lightly kissed her on the forehead and left the room. She was as confused now as she'd been at the river's edge. Her mother's words of encouragement, her hallucination of being a wolf, and her love making with Justin told her heart she knew deep inside exactly who she was. Everything her father told her was true, now if only her mind would accept the impossible.

***

"Justin?" Her eyes brimmed with tears and Justin took her in his arms. She was looking to him for answers, but he wasn't sure he had any more to give her.

"Don't let it worry you, Chas. In time you'll come to know, to accept." Justin rocked her gently in his arms like he would a small child. Once Chastity realized who she was and harnessed her morphing powers, it would be amazing.

As if the gates were suddenly open, sobs shook her body. Her uncontrollable weeping spilled out onto his shirt and all he could do was hold her until she quieted enough so he could tell her what he knew.

But could he tell her everything? There were many secrets the Langford family held close and hidden in their hearts. Justin didn't feel it was his place to tell her, not until there'd be no choice in the matter. For now, he had a choice.

At least the threat he'd thought existed on the shore was only a curious wolf. There were few white wolves in the area, in fact, there could only be one. Charles didn't seem too concerned about the stray wandering onto the company's property. It was soothing knowing it wasn't one of the Beta clan who'd met Chastity at the river.

He had his own demons to fight as well as watch over his mate. It wouldn't take long for Rowan to let his clan know that a Sinclair lived among the Langfords. Once that happened, all hell would break loose and blood would spill on both sides.

Chapter 12

Chastity punched her pillow for the hundredth time. The numbers of her alarm clock hadn't changed since the last time she checked the time. With all that had happened to her in the past twenty-four hours, she couldn't get her mind to settle down enough for her body to rest. Images of her family turning into wolves and back again kept their constant barrage on her psyche.

She wondered how they could have retained this from her all these years. But then again, how would they have explained to three little girls that they weren't really people, that they were animals of some kind. A smile seeped across her face. She imagined she and her sisters would have thought it was cool to be animals and not little girls. They would have tried to change every time they got mad at each other. Nope, it wouldn't have worked at all, and her parents sensed it.

She knew in her heart there was more to this than turning into wolves. Something told her lives were at stake, maybe more if her gut was right. *Daddy must have given me something that would explain everything, but what?*

Chastity paced back and forth at the foot of her bed, racking her brain for a lead. *The books! Those old books Daddy insisted I keep. There must be something there I can look at.*

Flashlight in hand, she crept into the living room, where Justin slept soundly on her sofa bed. She smiled, remembering how he'd insisted on staying with her after learning of her true heritage. Even as he slept, she believed he was protecting her in some way or another.

Edging her way past the sofa, Chastity turned on the small, battery-operated light and flashed it across the titles of the tattered leather volumes. Among classic titles like *Moby Dick*, *The Adventures of Tom Sawyer,* and *Dorian Gray* was a small, thin book titled *The Sinclairs*.

Her fingers trembled as she reached up and gently pulled the worn book from its hiding place. Nervous, scared, and excited, Chastity clicked off the light and tiptoed back to her bedroom.

She closed her bedroom door softly and then flipped on the switch to her bedside table lamp. Grabbing both her pillows and propping them against the headboard, Chastity crawled into bed.

Her heart beat rapidly against her rib cage, full of anticipation. Was everything in this one little volume? Would it be fact or fiction? Part of her wanted it to be the truth, while the scared little girl in her wanted it to be a story made to give kids nightmares. She began to read through the pages, hoping she'd find some answers to her far-too-many questions.

***

"We've got him, boys!" The deep words had more of a growl to them than a spoken language. Yipping and howling spun its way through the dark shadows of the trees. If he wasn't careful, they'd have him and that would be that. The sound of paws hitting the ground echoed through his mind, reminding him to pick up the pace; to lure them further from the ceremonial site.

His heart pounded through his chest, and with each breath he took, his lungs felt on fire. Why had he come to this god-forsaken country? He should have stayed home where he belonged, but didn't. Now he ran for his life, and the life of his yellow-eyed mate.

Their leader neared. He could smell his rancid breath. If he could only get to the clearing, into the light of the blue moon, he'd survive. He'd live to see his young grow for at least another year or two before they came hunting for him again, if at all.

The clearing was only a hundred yards in front of him. Almost home free! Faster, run faster, *he told himself, the ground feeling like nails under his pads. Fifty feet...twenty... A heavy weight fell on his back, knocking him to the ground. Fangs bared, he turned and sank his teeth into the leg of his attacker.*

Drool dripped from the Beta leader's mouth as he licked his lips. His movements slow and deliberate, Rowan Angus leaped onto his chest, pinning him to the ground. His eyes flashed red, and he howled his triumph, his fangs glowing in the night's...

"Noooooo!" Justin screamed, twisting and turning, trying to escape the sheets wrapped tightly around his legs.

"Shhhhh, it's okay Justin."

Chastity's soft voice filtered its way into the blackness surrounding his mind. Sweat seeped from every pore in his body, yet she held him close to her, calming him with her gentle rocking and soft murmuring.

"Shhhh. You're dreaming, Justin. It's only a dream, my love."

Her fingers swept through his hair and down his cheek over the tears that had slipped from his eyes. "Chas?"

"I'm here, have been all night." She kissed his forehead with a tenderness he'd never experienced before. The simple act sent a surge of warmth through his heart and soul, chasing away the demons.

Reaching up, he pulled her down to him, kissing every inch of her delectable body he had immediate access to and more. This woman, who he loved more than life itself, had no idea what her being next to him during the recurring nightmare meant to him. In that simple act, she'd become his salvation and safe haven.

Her body slid down next to his, every inch of her warm and inviting. He pinched a nipple as her breasts brushed against his chest, and she moaned her response. He ached to take her now before the glory of having her in his arms disappeared.

His body was being pushed flat against the mattress as she climbed on top of him. Her nightshirt bunched at her left hip, exposing the tuft of gold spun hair guarding the entrance to her cunt. She swung her hips across his, rubbing his cock between her pussy lips. Pulling her down to him, he kissed her deep and hard, tasting the sweetness of her mouth.

His rod thumped against the slickness of her clit, searching for the entrance that would give him the pleasure he knew waited for him. Pleasure that only he could have; pleasure that only she could give to him and no other.

Justin moaned into her mouth as she slid her cunt against the length of his hard shaft. He rubbed his hands down her back and over her ass, massaging each globe until it warmed under his hand. He lifted her hips slightly against him, and the head of his cock sprung into her opening. She slid down the length of it. Her muscles gripped him as she slid up then down until he felt he'd explode. Feeling her become hotter and her movements quicker, he knew she was on the brink of spilling her creamy juices all over him.

With one swift movement, he rubbed her ass and then slapped both cheeks, sending her cunt into convulsions. She moved quicker along his cock, a low growl escaped, and she came with the force of a rushing tide.

Her movement slowing, he rolled her over so she was on her knees in front of him. Her juices dripping from her, he slipped into her from behind, and drove but three times before he spilled his seed into her.

He collapsed onto her back, supporting the majority of his weight with his legs. Wrapping an arm around her, he pulled her close to him. He needed to feel her damp skin against his. Now if only he would live through the night of the blue moon to see his red-haired bride grow old and grey, he'd consider himself a hell of a lucky man.

***

Chastity stretched along the length of the man she loved, regardless of who he was. After reading the book, coupled with the nightmare Justin had, she believed she'd read his life story on those browned pages. There was no doubt in her mind the Justin Matthews who lay gloriously naked beside her, was the Remington Sinclair in that tattered old book. Or he'd been lucky enough to have his ancestor's drop dead good looks.

She ran her hands over his muscled biceps and onto his chest, her fingers mingling with the black hairs circling his nipples.

"Mmmm, I'll give you a lifetime to stop doing that."

She continued circling a beaded nipple, "Is that all...a lifetime? I was hoping for something like eternity." she teased, licking the hardened peak.

He stretched and wrapped his legs around hers. "Whatever you wish, Princess."

"Whatever?" She licked at his nipple, circling

it with her tongue.

"God, yes, whatever." He pulled her up to him, kissing her full on the lips. His hands moved over her ass and he held her closer to him.

"As tempting as feeling you inside me may be, all I want right now is to know everything about you." Chastity snuggled next to him, inhaling the muskiness of his skin.

"I'm afraid my life's a little boring."

"Well," Chastity rolled over and reached to the floor, "not according to this it isn't." She waved the old leather volume in the air. "Come on, Matthews, admit it. Maybe I should call you Sinclair instead."

"Shit." Justin sat up in bed, looking at her as if she'd just made up some sort of fairy tale that had come true.

She leaned up to kiss his cheek. "The jig's up and you know it. Now spill your guts." She settled down next to him, taking his hand in hers. She wanted to make sure he knew she supported him now and forever. She wanted him to tell her his side without any pressure or consequences. She was his no matter what, and if he didn't know it by now, he would before long.

He sighed deeply, his stomach muscles quivering. "You've read the book then?"

She kissed the palm of his hand, tracing the center of it with her tongue. "Yes, my love. But I want to hear it from you, not read about it in the pages of a centuries old book."

"You know everything, what more is there?" He held her next to him, as though if he didn't, she'd run away. She knew there was more to him than what she'd read, she just wanted to hear it from him.

She sat up next to him, drinking in the wonder of his gold-speckled eyes. "Not everything, Justin."

He pushed to a sitting position, placing a couple of the pillows behind him. He looked like a child about to give away his deepest, darkest secret and she guessed that's exactly what he was going to do.

"There's really not much more to tell. I'm a direct descendant of English werewolves. Some say I'm the reincarnation of Remington himself." He laughed as a tear seeped out of the corner of his eye. "And who's to say I'm not? All I know is that when I was three, you were promised to me as you left your mother's womb. Since then, there are a great many things I must do in this lifetime, Chastity. One of them being your protector, your friend, and your mate."

"And what are the other things that are so important that you'd risk your life for them?" Chastity fought back the tears threatening to find their way into her eyes. She'd learned quite a bit from that little book, and a werewolf putting their life on the line for something was just one.

Justin held her hand tightly in his. She never wanted him to let go. She was afraid that if he did, he'd shut her out and run far from her.

"The Beta clan has a couple of items that belong to me." His warm, golden eyes turned cold. He looked past her shoulder to the dawn peeking through the blinds. "One is my cousin,

Lucas Kendal, and the other is the pelt and remains of Remington Sinclair."

Chapter 13

The coldness of dread seeped its way through Justin's veins. He didn't know if Chastity could ever fully understand the depths of his soul. There was a blackness so horrifying that if allowed to surface uncontrolled, it would be the end for him...and their life together.

Since the day he'd been born, his family believed he was Remington Sinclair come to avenge his untimely death in the Americas. Justin didn't believe it for a minute; what he did believe was that he'd been sent to take back what rightfully belonged to the Elites. Once he did, what remained of Remington's body could be properly buried and put to rest, and Lucas would belong where he did, with his true family.

Justin turned his attention back to Chastity, giving her a lingering kiss. "Remember the other day after your father found us in—"

"Ah, yeah, just go on." Her yellow eyes sparkled and her cheeks paled a soft shade of pink before she shyly looked away.

Damn, she's even more beautiful when she's

embarrassed. "Anyway, we were discussing a plan to rescue Lucas from the Beta camp. Your father's been working on this for several years with some of the clan undercover in less than desirable conditions. A breakthrough came a few months ago, and with the blue moon on the rise, he summoned me to his side."

Confusion raced across her face, leaving a trace of fear in its path. "When, when is this supposed to happen?"

He sighed long and deep. "Before the binding ceremony, when they won't be expecting our warriors." He hated to tell her like this, but as usual, he'd been left with no choice. And so much for romantic notions that didn't have a chance to materialize.

She traced a circle around his belly button, sending hot liquid through him. If she kept it up, there'd be no more answers to her questions. He'd be far too busy making love to her.

"So, what's a binding ceremony anyway?" She bent, sucked his belly button, and woke his cock from its nap.

"Ohhh," he moaned, reaching for her. "It's a ceremony performed when the blue moon is at its highest in the night sky. I guess you could call it a wolfen wedding of sorts."

Her fingers feathered along his jaw line, and he felt his focus slip away. "And just who is supposed to be at this ceremony? That is, if there's anyone left to attend after you go on that gang fight on the other side of the river."

He sucked her finger as she slipped it into his mouth then pulled it from him. "Geez,

Chastity, do you have to do that? I can barely think anymore." He rolled her over and took a nipple in his mouth. He'd waited long enough to taste her again, and she'd been teasing him far longer than he could withstand.

She arched into him, filling his mouth with her breast. Beneath him, her legs spread and wrapped themselves around his hips. His cock thumped against the hot, wet opening to her pleasure zone. He felt her shift slightly and then pull his hips down onto her. His rock hard shaft slipped into her juices. Before he could think, she was moving her hips against him, urging him to dance with her.

"Tell me, Justin," she whispered, moving and grinding beneath him.

"What?" He wasn't sure exactly what she wanted to know. Was it more about the binding ceremony or who would be attending? Or did she want to hear she was driving him beyond rational thought with her movements?

Her legs pulled him tighter and her hips moved quicker. "Is this what the binding ceremony is like, Justin?"

"In a way and only if asked." He moved with her, his cock pulsed, near bursting with cum to be released.

She gripped him tighter. Her juices were hotter and wetter the faster he fucked her pussy. Her muscles contracted around him, and his cum burst from its holding chamber. She kept her legs wrapped around him, sucking his cock with her cunt until her cum mingled with his.

He caught his breath and looked down into

her sweat-drenched face. She was one hell of a beautiful woman no matter what condition she was in. If he didn't make her his, he couldn't see living another minute without her.

"Marry me, Chastity," he said, kissing every inch of her face.

***

What? Justin's continuing kissing of her face made it hard to focus on what he'd just said. *Did he just ask me to marry him? Or was it wishful thinking?*

He took her hand in his and kissed each of her fingertips. "Did you just...?"

"Ask you to marry me?" he said, a sweet smile on his face. His eyes were full of warmth and love and she thought she'd gone to heaven.

"Ah, something like that." She watched him interlock their fingers together, becoming one with the other. Tears welled up in her eyes at the question that she was about to answer. *I can't believe it. He must be serious or he wouldn't bring it up again.*

"I'll only ask you once, Chastity and that was it." He licked, and then kissed her lips with tenderness.

"Yes, Justin. I'll marry you," she answered, giggling as tears spilled from her eyes. "When?"

"Tonight, when the blue moon is at its highest in the night sky. Then and only then will we truly be as we were meant to be." Justin trailed kisses down her belly, sending goose bumps of desire through her.

"But, what about—"

Knock, knock!

"Justin!" Her father's voice boomed through her front door, knocking her back to the reality of Justin's earlier words of a gang war. She pulled the sheet up over her body, covering her nakedness as much as she could.

She wanted to ask Justin why her father was there, but she already knew. The time had come for them to do what they had to do. The bride-to-be would be left at the altar wondering if her groom would be returning to her.

***

Not now, Charles. Justin looked at the tears in Chastity's eyes. A few minutes ago he would have thought what were from happiness was the opposite now. He slipped away from her, yanked up his pants, and walked across the floor to answer the door. He hadn't expected the time for battle to come so soon.

Pulling it open, he let Charles into his daughter's apartment. "Chastity, I'm sorry to do this. We...I need Justin to come with me."

Justin slid his shirt over his head, tucking it into the waistband of his jeans. "She knows, Charles. I wouldn't recommend lying right now."

Charles nodded. "Okay, we don't have long."

Justin took a seat next to Chastity and wiped away the tears trailing down her cheeks. "I'll be there, on time and in one piece." *If there is a God for creatures like us, I pray that you let me return to her.* He kissed her deep, letting her know that he would be true to his word. "I've got to go now."

He walked to where Charles stood just inside the doorway. "Let's get it done, then."

Charles walked past him, stopping just inside the opening. He turned to look at his daughter's tear-stained face. "As God as my witness, I'll make sure he comes back in one piece."

Justin's heart pounded in his chest, fear had an iron grip on his soul. If they failed tonight, their carcasses could end up another trophy for Rowan and the Beta clan. Failure wasn't an option for any of them this night, or any other night.

Looking away from Chastity, he walked out and closed the door behind him. "You shouldn't make such promises, Charles. And you damn well know God has nothing to do with this."

Charles stomped down the hallway of Chastity's apartment building. "Whatever you want to believe in. Right now we've got to get our warriors together and discuss our strategy. If we're to do this before the moon is at its highest, we've got to move now, not six hours from now."

Justin caught up to him, pushing open the door to the outside world. "Once everyone's briefed and we're on our way I'll feel better. You know my mission is two-fold, Charles. Once Lucas is freed, I'll be heading to Rowan's to reclaim what doesn't belong to him."

"We've got that covered too. You won't be going in alone." Charles stopped Justin, looking him square in the eye. "I'm going. I've known Rowan for a good many years. If need be, I know how to reason with him...and what his weak points are."

Anger raced through Justin. He'd be damned if Charles thought he'd go along with that hair-brained idea. "Damn it, Charles! You'll not risk your life for my ancestor's remains. That part of the fight is mine and no one else's. There'll be enough blood spilled tonight. I'll not have more because—"

"Who in the hell do you think you are, Justin? Just because you're a direct bloodline doesn't mean the clan doesn't know what it means to put Remington to rest. We may be a damned lot, but we've got a great tradition and know exactly where, and who, we all came from."

Chapter 14

Chastity didn't know how long she'd been asleep. Her head pounded, and her eyes felt swollen from crying. The room grew dark as the sun set in the west. The coming night held deathly quiet. It was like the quiet before the storm she'd heard her parents refer to so many times in her life. Now she knew what they meant.

"You mustn't worry, Chastity. Everything will be as it should, nothing you do will ever change that." Her mother's voice wafted from the chair next to the sofa. From the looks of it, she'd been there for quite some time, for she looked to be settled in pretty well.

"Oh, Mama." She wiped the tears spilling down her cheeks. "What if he doesn't come back? I could never love another for as long as I live." She shivered from the chill running through her that never seemed to leave. "I've never been so cold in my life. It's like everything I've ever believed in is lost."

Joanna got up from the chair and sat next to her. She pulled the blanket around Chastity and held her close. The last time she was in her mother's arms was after her beloved pony had broken a leg and had to be put down. She'd thought her world had ended then; she guessed in a way, some small part of it had, leaving room for new growth.

"Ah, but not all is lost. Tonight is your wedding night, and we've got much preparation to do." Joanna kissed her cheek and then left her side.

Chastity willed herself off the sofa bed. "How can there be when I don't even know if the groom will be alive?" She stood looking out over the river into the Brey Forest where the men she loved were getting ready to wage battle. She supposed rescuing Lucas Kendal was a good enough reason, if any. Maybe she'd come to understand Justin's other reason, in time.

"Come, daughter, we don't have as much time as you think we do." Joanna held her apartment door open. She clutched Chastity's purse in one hand and her set of keys in the other.

Chastity shuffled over to her mother, dropping the blanket in a heap on the sofa. If nothing else, once this was over and she was left a widow before she'd been married, she'd have that sofa, the sheets, and the scent of their love-making to keep her warm for the rest of her life.

***

The snarling and howling continued around Justin as he waited in the woods. The battle sounds would forever be imbedded in a dark section of his memory. They'd found where Lucas had been held captive, losing a number of lives along the way.

"What the hell are you doing?" Justin whispered in anger as Charles hunkered down next to him. He'd thought he'd slipped away without the Elite leader noticing. He should have known better than to believe Charles had been paying attention to the fighting instead of his whereabouts.

"Now that Lucas is safe, I've got another family member to return home in one piece," he said, catching his breath. He looked worn out and about to collapse on the spot, but there was nothing Justin could do about it now. Charles had committed himself.

"How many more casualties?" Justin watched the woods surrounding Rowan's cabin. He knew the pelt was there, he could almost smell it through the animal and human waste soaked into the ground. How they could live in such filth was beyond him. The Betas lived like the animals they were, surrounded by filth and disease and decay.

Charles gripped his arm and squeezed. "Unknown...Lash is hurt. Lucas is with him and will get him back to our clan for care."

"Damn it!" There was nothing he could do about it now. It would be a tragedy to lose a family member while trying to save another, but that was the nature of going to war. Lives were lost while others were spared. There was no rhyme or reason; war was as it was.

"There's been no sign of Rowan, but I don't

trust him not to be lurking somewhere nearby."
Justin began the morphing transformation from
human to werewolf. "You keep watch out here
while I go inside that toilet of a place Rowan calls
home. If you see anyone, yip like a coyote, and
then get the hell out of here."

Justin took off through the trees to the
house, his wolf senses on high alert. He wasn't
about to give Charles a chance to object, not with
so much on the line. If Charles didn't return to
the compound, there'd be a full-blown war
between the clans.

He circled around the back to the front of the
building, sniffing as he went. *This is worse than
I could ever imagine. It'll take a year to get the
stench off of Lucas, or any of us for that matter.*

He peeked through window, barely able to
see through the layers of grime. Across the room,
above the fireplace, hung a black wolf pelt with a
skull in a glass enclosure on the mantle.

Justin's heart fell like an elevator out of
control. *Remington Sinclair!*

He pushed open the cabin door with his
snout, morphed back to his human form, and
walked upright into the sparsely furnished room.
Focusing on the reclaiming of the pelt and
remains, Justin pushed the pain of changing so
quickly from his mind and paused in front of the
fireplace. Without a moment's hesitation, he
lifted the skull from its enclosure and placed it in
the pouch hanging from his hip. Securing the
pouch, he reached up and pulled the pelt from
the wall.

Coyote yipping came from the woods, and he

wrapped the black fur around his shoulders, securing it with a leather tether. Justin walked out the door with caution, returning to all fours and changing back to a wolf as he ran from the cabin.

The yipping continued three more times, a signal that Charles was still alive. But he couldn't worry about that right now, he had to get out of the woods and back to the other side of the river. The Elite warriors would be on their way back, bloody and wounded, but most of them would return alive.

Justin ran top speed through the woods. He could feel the Beta leader closing in on him, and with the weight of the pelt and pouch, Justin knew Rowan would gain ground on him quickly. Hopefully he was far enough ahead that it wouldn't matter. He picked up speed, even though the ground felt like nails being driven into the pads of his paws.

He only had about twenty more feet, and he'd be in the clearing where the blue moon spread its rays across the meadow. Just ahead, through the break in the forest, he could see the clearing that lay beyond trees.

A great weight hit his back and he fell to the ground.

"You spoiled bastard! How dare you believe you can come into our camp and—"

Baring his fangs, Justin turned and planted his teeth into Rowan Angus's leg. Rowan howled and then stood upright, face to face with Justin. Rowan leaped at Justin, his eyes as red as the blood dripping from his teeth.

"Noooo!" Justin howled into the night, before everything became a blur. The pelt melted from his body and the pouch fell empty at his side. Standing between him and Rowan was the greatest wolfen either clan had ever known...Remington Sinclair.

***

"Isn't it beautiful, Chastity?" Charity pulled their mother's wedding gown from the storage box. "I still can't believe you're getting married, and in the middle of the night too. I hope this guy's worth it."

Chastity turned from the bunker window and pasted a happy smile on her face. "So do I, Chari." She'd be a hundred times happier if only Justin would return safe and sound.

"Mother's dress fits you perfectly, you know. It's simple, with no frills, and very elegant. When, no, make that *if*, I ever get married, I want to look like a princess going to the ball." Charity laid their mother's dress out across the bed next to the simple wreath of lavender and blue starflowers.

Chastity hadn't had the heart to argue with her mother about tonight. She'd much rather have waited in the appointed spot for Justin to arrive...pure and simple. What they had between them was more than pretty dresses, fancy flowers, and music playing gaily through the night.

"Come on, girls. We've got a wedding to get dressed for!" Joanna breezed into the room without a care in the world. Chastity wondered how she managed to go on like nothing was happening on the other side of the river in the depths of the forest.

There'd been no word, and it drove her crazy. She wanted to know if Justin, her father, and the others were alive or not. She wanted to know that the man she loved would return to her when the moon reached its highest peak. She wanted to know if she'd spend the rest of her life in solitude.

"Chastity." Her father's voice warmed her skin. "You're getting married in less than an hour. I don't think you want to leave the groom standing at the altar, do you?"

Her heart raced with jubilation. "Daddy!" She threw her arms around her father, hugging him close to her. "You're alive!" She stepped away, her heart ceasing to beat one more time. "Justin?"

Her father's weak smile pummeled her heart to the floor. Her worst fear began to mist over her soul, but she had to ask, had to know...was he alive?

Charles pulled her to him, holding her close. "He awaits his bride."

Epilogue

With the blue moon at its highest in the night sky, and the meadow awash with blue moonlight, all the blood and death from the Brey Forest was forgotten. Instead, the binding destiny of the red-haired princess and the black European wolf was taking place for the first time in centuries by the blue moon.

Chastity was never happier in her life as she was when her mother placed the wreath on her head. The mix of the lavender and blue starflowers almost as intoxicating as knowing that, in just a few minutes, she'd be married to one Justin Matthew Sinclair.

Floating down the aisle, formed of Elite clan members with her sisters in tow, Chastity kept her eyes on Justin, afraid that if she didn't, he'd disappear from her sight. Tears welled up in her eyes, and her father handed her a lace hanky. She couldn't be happier...both the men in her life were alive and she couldn't love either of them more.

"Who gives away this bride?"

"Her mother and I do," her father announced to the clan, his voice a bit shaky and a tear of joy slipping down his cheek.

Charles handed Chastity over to Justin, holding their hands together for a lingering moment. "You better give her nothing less than your life, son."

Justin nodded in acknowledgement. The words, although warm and loving, were a warning to do right by Chastity.

"I love you, Daddy." Chastity whispered so only the three of them could hear.

"And I you, daughter." He placed his hand upon her cheek before taking his seat next to Joanna.

"Let the binding ceremony begin." The minister took Chastity's and Justin's hands in his own and then wrapped a leather tether around their wrists. "You may say your vows of promise to one another."

Justin turned to Chastity, his gold-specked eyes full of warmth and love. "The star on your forehead says that you are mine to love and cherish for all eternity. My heart is your place of warmth and my soul, your sanctuary. Know that I will also love and protect you for as long as this world allows me." Justin reached into his pocket, in order to place the most beautiful ring she'd ever seen on her finger. "Chastity Lynne Langford, the star sapphire ring on your finger is a symbol of our destiny to be one."

Tears flowed down her cheeks as the ring slipped over her knuckle and settled into its place with ease.

"You are my heart and my soul, matching mating stars or not. I will also be there for you to lean on when the times are rough and to laugh with in happier times. Know that I will always love and protect you for as long as this world allows me." Chastity took the wide band with a star sapphire to match hers from Charity. Looking into his eyes, she began to slide it on his finger. "Justin Matthew Sinclair, the star sapphire ring on your finger is a symbol of our destiny to be one."

"The binding ceremony has been completed. Chastity Lynne Langford and Justin Matthew Sinclair have declared their love and are mates for a lifetime."

Chastity fell into Justin's arms, feeling safe and loved by a man she'd once despised; a wolfen who, like her, had found his place in the world.

THE END

About the Author

Although some like to think **Ms. Wilder** lives what she writes, it's far from the truth. She has shelves filled with research books such as *Sex Toy Tales, Lip Service*, and *The Academy,* which she gets from her sister-in-law from time to time. Thankfully, her husband doesn't think they have to try everything at least once!

Ms. Wilder loves the freedom that writing erotica brings. There's a no holds barred attitude that suits her when her imagination and characters take over and run wild on the pages. And like her characters, she believes romance and sex go hand in hand.

She currently lives a quiet life with her husband, nestled deep among the pyramids of Rock Lake.

By the Blue Moon is the final print book available by **Ms. Wilder** a/k/a Maxine Douglas.

Praise for Debi Wilder's Books:

Gabby's Second Chance
5.0 out of 5 stars
Wilder does it AGAIN!
By Carol C. MacLeod
What a wonderful story about love and loss. How many of us have experienced it as deeply as Gabby Adams and forgiven ourselves?

This is a heartfelt story told by the talented author Debi Wilder and should be on the "must read" list for everyone whose heart has been bruised by making a mistake with love. This woman did the unthinkable and believes herself unforgiveable.

Not only does Gabby find forgiveness, but she finds she is truly worthy of love. This one is a tear jerker and bound to make you want to read even more of this fantastic author!

Awards:

2006 ~ EPIC eBook Award for Best Anthology of the Year for *Tales of the Treasure Trove*, a Jewels of the Quill Anthology.

You can find more on **Debi Wilder** and her books at:

Her Blog
http://authordebiwilder.blogspot.com/

Follow her on Twitter
@waMaxineDouglas

A Sneak Peek

Twice in A Blue Moon
By
Honey Jans

Book 2
Blue Moon Magic

Charity Langford has a secret passion. Lucas Kendal has promises to keep. When the budding were-princess and hired gun meet, sparks fly.

Charity Langford rushed back to her office in the Langford and Langford IT department, cheeks flaming. Good heavens! She'd just confirmed that at least one of the Langford sisters was getting laid on a regular basis. But really, catching Chas and Justin making love in the executive washroom was just plain embarrassing, not that they seemed to notice her presence or care, for that matter.

She was the one with issues, according to her older sister. But this breach of conduct was way over the line. Even worse, it forcefully brought home to her the sex she wasn't having. She rolled her eyes at her own pity party, conceding that she was overreacting. But at least she had the good grace to keep her sex life, pure fantasy though it was, private.

No one needed to know how much she'd come to crave her daily visits to Dominion.net, and she sure as shooting wasn't about to share her Cyber Laird, so sexually dominant he could make her come from afar with a few keystrokes, with anyone. Just thinking of him made her body pulse with heat and kicked her senses into sharp focus as she heard her staff gossiping in the other room, and damn if she didn't smell cinnamon rolls in the cafeteria. It was all because of her way-too-vivid imagination, she knew, but it seemed otherworldly and even scary. Now who was overreacting? She rolled her eyes again.

But wait. Hadn't Chastity complained of similar sensory sensations when she and Justin hooked up? And even more potently in Charity's mind, her Laird was able to do it to her wirelessly, turning her into a super geek in the computer lab. A wry smile twisted her lips. The man must pack a whopping load of testosterone to affect her this way.

Passing her sometimes-too-nosy staff, as their gossip abruptly died down, she tried to downplay the fact that she was aroused. Since the attempted hacking attack to her server two weeks back, her staff had acted far more protectively than she liked, probably on her father's orders. He'd been on edge since she'd hit the hackers with her proprietary fireball program, frying their systems from afar, and they'd struck back at her with empty threats. Consequently, her dad had gone completely overboard and hired a nasty, drop dead sexy guard dog of a PI.

She studiously avoided eye contact with said bodyguard—Lucas A. Kendal, PI extraordinaire, according to her dad—as she attempted to breeze past him. Still, she couldn't resist taking a peek. Longish dark hair that curled around the collar of his black tee shirt, sharp whiskey brown eyes that didn't miss a thing, and a sexy body made for sin; he made her heart race just looking at him. The calculating gaze the dark-eyed stud ran over her focused on her blush and told her he sensed what she'd seen, and her heated reaction to it.

The corner of his hard mouth quirked up in a heartbreaker's grin that made her wet in ten seconds flat, even as it made her want to deck him. If *screw you* could have been conveyed by a look, she shot it back at him. Unfortunately, her displeasure didn't seem to faze him one little bit, the Alpha-male jerk.

He stayed at his post, sprawled in a desk chair across from her private office, where he could keep an eye on her, according to him. *"You're not going to give me the slip, sweetheart. Try it again and pay the penalty,"* he'd warned the first time she'd attempted to get away and he'd caught her in the elevator.

Pressed into a corner as he loomed over her, his body heat making her burn, she'd damned near melted. She hadn't dared to ask what the penalty was. Based on his dominant gaze, she had a pretty good idea it involved her bent over his knee. What a Neanderthal. But she couldn't help creaming as the rock hard proof of his arousal pressed against her. Then he leaned in to sniff her neck, and she fluttered inside as he let out a low, primal growl. When an equally primitive growl poured out of her, it seemed to shock both of them as he drew back to look at her.

Time had stood still as he stared at her mouth, and she leaned forward, puckering up for a kiss. The elevator doors dinged open, he backed off with a curse, and she sagged against the railing, all stirred up for nothing. Thank heavens she'd found the link for Dominion that night, or she might have tried to do something drastic, like knock him to the floor and do him.

Now there he sat, dressed in black jeans that fit him like a second skin, and a black tee shirt defining all his muscled glory in defiance of the company dress code. The work she'd assigned him as a cover sat there, completely ignored. He stared at her like he owned her—and knew she wasn't wearing underwear. Hellfire, it was a wonder he hadn't followed her into the ladies room to find out. The thought sent quivers through her sex.

Cut it out, she scolded herself, squeezing her thighs together to stop the sensual fluttering down below. It was impossible. The man practically oozed sex appeal. Her lips tingled as she stared at him, focusing on his sultry mouth. What might he taste like? She was dying to find out; maybe nibble his square jaw and dip her tongue into that cute cleft in his chin. *Down, girl. He's here to look after you, not teach you the joys of sex at your old-maid age of thirty-two.* His quirked brow told her he guessed the sexual nature of her thoughts.

Cheeks flaming anew, she escaped to her office, quickly shutting the door and locking it. Thank goodness she had her cyber laird to dim the flames and help her refocus. This maddening, sexual itch, combined with the series of hacking attacks she'd thwarted, threatened to drive her crazy. Ending the barrage of attacks with her special fireball program had made enemies. The pissed-off hackers sent death threats, prompting her father to hire Kendal, who made her want to knock him to the floor and jump his bones. It was a vicious cycle, one she couldn't seem to break. But maybe, at the IT conference in Vegas, she could find someone who…

Sighing at her wishful thinking, she peeled off the jacket of her business suit, loving the way her silk blouse felt against her bare skin, and rushed over to her computer, late for a date with her cyber master. She had two hours until she had to leave for her staff's annual weekend getaway to the IT Conference. A weekend far away from her annoying babysitter would be wonderful. Maybe she could actually hook up with a charming stranger in Las Vegas, sow a few wild oats, and get this desire for sex out of her system.

She slipped into her desk chair and reached for her computer's keyboard. Her excitement building, she logged onto Dominion.net and looked for his screen name. Yes! He was there. *Wolf*. A thrill went through her. She logged on as *Sugar*, and put on her headset, saying softly, *"I'm here, my laird."*

"Follow me to our private room, Sugar."

She shivered, hearing his sexy rumble; a thick brogue that rushed over her like a warm caress, causing her sex to cream as she imagined what was coming. Sex with a guy wearing a kilt—now that inspired all kinds of kinky possibilities, ones she was dying to explore if ever he'd agree to meet her for real. So far, she'd struck out with him too.

With guilty pleasure, she murmured. *"Yes, my laird."* Maybe it was better this way. She could surrender to her online master, get off, and still maintain an illusion of icy reserve in public.

"How many times did you touch yourself today, Sugar?"

His blunt demand made her hesitate, a blush heating her face. As a redhead, she hated her inability to lie, because her blushes always gave her away. Hell, her laird wouldn't know one way or another. After a tense, weighted moment of self-recrimination, she let out a sigh of surrender.

Here comes the Langford upbringing again...Finish what you start and never lie to anyone about anything, period. Sighing, she confessed, *"Six times, my laird."* His chuckle made her squirm in her office chair. She was going to get punished but good, and anticipation made her tingle all over. She thought about the vibrator in her desk drawer. Maybe he'd make her come three times in a row like last time.

"What a naughty girl, not to wait for your master's permission."

His scolding echoed her thoughts. Why couldn't she control herself? It had been so easy two weeks ago, but Kendal's presence had seemed to trip an invisible switch inside her, bringing her wanton sexuality to the surface. *"I'm sorry, sir."* She shivered with delight, getting into the secret fantasy. Thankfully, it was just the two of them and Kendal never need know.

"Did you obey my instructions, Sugar?"

She brushed her bare breasts though her silk blouse, loving the free, sensual feeling of forgoing her usual bra and panties. "*Yes, laird, I'm not wearing any underwear.*"

He took in a deep breath. "*Good girl. Unbutton your blouse for me, and play with your sexy tits, bad girl.*"

She shuddered, a thrill going through her at his explicit words, meant to turn her on, she was sure. "*Yes, my laird.*" Her hands quickly flew to do his bidding. She slipped the ivory buttons of her white silk blouse out of their buttonholes until the teasing garment hung open. The air conditioning wafted a cool breeze over her budding nipples, and she shivered with delight. She bit back a whimper as her nipples tightened.

With a sigh of pleasure, she cupped her full breasts and fanned her fingertips over the exquisitely hard peaks, murmuring at the pleasure as she stimulated them again in his direction. He'd practically worn her out in the last week, sending her sex toys, having her try the most shocking things on her sexually awakening body. She pinched her nipples, rolling them. "*I'm playing with them, my laird.*"

"*Excellent. Imagine it's my big hands touching them, getting your tasty nipples nice and hard for me.*"

Closing her eyes, she pictured her mystery laird, imagining her soft hands becoming his larger, harder ones, his rougher fingertips rolling her stiff nipples firmly, tugging on them. "*My nipples are so very hard for you, laird.*"

"*Now pinch them for me, Sugar, a small punishment for being late.*"

She pinched them firmly, whimpering at the

erotic feeling that shot through her, making her sex clench.

"Good girl. Now spread your legs and touch your pussy. Let me know if it's wet for me."

She sighed in willing surrender, leaning back in her big desk chair, and spread her legs, her hand reaching under her skirt to touch her hot pussy. Her clit was stiff and distended, tingling like a million nerve endings were on fire for him, her pussy quivering and wet... She sobbed...sadly, it was also empty. Damn it, she needed him. Still, she rubbed her clit for him like the good little submissive he was turning her into, moaning uncontrollably. *"I'm very wet, sir."*

"Good. Play with that bad pussy, make it nice and creamy for me, but don't you dare come, Sugar."

She stroked her wet slit, her thumb rubbing her stiff clit as she registered his stern command. Not come...that was impossible, and well he knew it. Still, she couldn't hold back a moan as she got nearer to orgasm.

"Imagine it's my hand touching you, my fingers slipping inside your wet pussy, getting you ready to be fucked."

She bit her lip on a shaky breath at the F-word, her fingers plunging into her damp sex with a lewd, wet sound she was sure he detected. His sexy growl confirmed she was right. *"Yes, my laird. I'm imagining it's you. When can we meet for real?"* she asked, desperate for a taste of the real thing. Heck, for all she knew, he could be anyone, maybe some dirty old man. She had to find out. And if he didn't make good on these preliminaries, she was going to explode.

"When I think you're ready, honey, and not before."

She groaned at his brusque rejection, but it didn't stop her hot response to his commands, or her growing need for him.

"Do you like the way it feels when my fingers plunge inside you, filling you?"

She panted, her pussy clenching on her fingers as he spoke. *"Oh yes, laird, very much."*

"Now stop."

Trembling, on the brink of a huge orgasm, her fingers went still at his command. *"Please, sir."*

"No. You're being punished for playing with yourself earlier. I'll talk to you tomorrow."

Charity moaned as he disconnected and tried to stop like he'd commanded. She really did, but there was no way of stopping her impending volcanic eruption of an orgasm. He'd gotten her too used to them, too needy.

Her reckless fingers plunged into her wet pussy, pretending they were her mystery laird's, and she groaned, tightening herself around them, trying to imagine they were his cock. *His cock!* Oh god, it tripped her trigger, and she cried out as her wet sex convulsed, and she exploded into orgasm. She was dimly aware of her office door opening as she came like an out of control bitch in heat.

***

Lucas Kendal stood inside Charity

Langford's office doorway, blocking anyone passing by from ogling his beautiful she-wolf mate in the throes of passion. *Oh lord!* His cock surged forward inside his suddenly too tight jeans, torturing him, but he couldn't look away. Still shaken by the culture shock of being rescued by the Elite, only to have his half-brother Lash killed in the raid, he was still trying to get his bearings. Going around like a randy wolf in heat for the first time wasn't helping him stay in control.

The cyber-sex he'd initiated to get sweet, sexy-as-hell Charity ready for mating with him had backfired big time. Consequently, he was frustrated, horny as hell, and pissed off in general. But he would not be deterred from bedding her. The problem was keeping his promise to take Lash's place as Charity's mate while not succumbing to her charms. Claiming her was going to be harder than he'd thought, because he wouldn't get to keep her.

It wasn't all *that was hard*, he thought ruefully, stroking his cock's raging shaft through his jeans. Good lord, she was killing him. He hadn't been able to resist cornering her in the elevator, getting drunk on her sweet, alluring pheromones as he'd scented her blatantly, sniffing her while pressing his cock against her creamy wetness. It made her gasp and pucker up like she expected him to kiss her, shocking the hell out of him. That's when he'd cursed himself, pulled back. He'd regretted it ever after. Since then, she'd eyed him like the animal he was. Smart girl.

Didn't matter. He'd do what he had to in order to protect her; teach her about passion, sex, and who she was before she dumped him. He was no more than a stud for hire, after all, and it was his role in life. Hell, he ought to be used to it after the Beta's breeding farm.

After the danger of the blue moon was past for Charity, her father would choose a more suitable husband for her from among the Elites, and Lucas would travel on; ever moving in the shadowy world of the Alphas. His feelings, if he even had any, didn't matter. Still, he couldn't help watching her in the throes of an orgasm he'd initiated, feeling like a needy whelp with his first mate.

Charity's pretty face was flushed with passion, her headset still in place, her eyes shut, as the extended orgasm swept her away. His hunter's gaze focused hungrily on her beautiful, bare breasts, the tasty stiff nipples like ripe red strawberries. How he ached to taste them for real. The sweet sounds of ecstasy pouring from her full red lips was like music to his ears, and would be like catnip to any rogue wolf within a sixty-yard radius. This was no longer about a turf war between wolfen societies. From the moment he'd met her two weeks ago, this had turned very personal.

What a naughty girl to disobey him and keep playing with herself. He'd have to spank her for it eventually. He knew she'd love it. She was so exquisitely responsive, it was hard for him to restrain his dominant, sexual animal instincts. He itched to take her over his knee in retribution and then make love to her until she couldn't think straight, couldn't deny him.

"Want me to take care of that for you, love?" he asked, working hard to keep the sound of his Scots ancestry out of his voice. It wouldn't do for her to guess that he and her "laird" were one and the same. He watched her big violet eyes pop open.

Lucas smiled as her mouth formed a perfect "O" of shock, but true to her royal status, her dismay soon was replaced by an imperious glare as she stared back at him, her fingers still stroking her wet pussy. He could smell her scent from across the room, and his rod hardened in response, lengthening as her startled, maybe fascinated, gaze watched it happen. Hell, yeah, he had what she needed, but first, she'd have to obey him.

"Who gave you a key to my office?" she demanded, pulling her hand out from under her skirt and buttoning her blouse.

He kicked shut the door behind him and held up his bare hands. "Look, doll, no key. The door was unlocked." He didn't bother mentioning that his fully developed skills gave him powers she'd never dreamed of; opening a locked door was dead easy. He'd walk through fire to get to her and keep her safe. She just didn't know it yet.

He closed the distance between them, noting her trembling hands as she finished buttoning her blouse. The lady wasn't as unperturbed as she pretended to be. Good. It suited him to keep her off balance. "We need to talk about this weekend."

"Save your breath, Kendal, I'm going."

"Have it your way," he murmured, focusing on her stiff nipples showing clearly through her silk blouse. "I'll have to go with you."

Noting the direction of his stare, she scowled and swiveled her desk chair so that her back was to him, stood, and put on her blazer. "I'll see you at the airport, then."

"It doesn't work that way and you know it. I've arranged transport for us. I'll be here to collect you in half an hour," he said, turning to walk out of the room. For all his sexual experience, he couldn't help feeling like the vulnerable one.

Dear Reader,

I hope you enjoyed **By the Blue Moon**. I have to tell you, I really love the characters of Chastity and Justin. Many readers wrote me asking: "What's next for them? What about their family and life together? Will Chastity and Justin have any children, and what powers will they have? Will the Betas seek revenge on Justin for apparently killing Rowen Angus? And what of Langford and Langford? Will Justin take over the reins or defy his Beta leader and father-in-law?" Well, stay tuned as my Blue Moon world continues. They'll all be back in **Blue Moon Justice** coming in 2015. Will there be a happy ending? Wait and see.

When I wrote **By the Blue Moon**, I got so many letters from fans thanking me for the book. As an author, I love feedback. Frankly, you are the reason that I write. So, tell me what you liked, what you loved, even what you hated. I'd love to hear from you. You can write me at debiwilder@gmail.com and visit me on the web at http://authordebiwilder.blogspot.com.

Finally, I need to ask a favor, if you're so inclined I'd love a review of **By the Blue Moon**. Loved it, hated it, whatever you really think—I'd just enjoy your feedback.

As you might know, reviews can be tough to come by these days. You, the reader, have the power now to make or break a book, or an author. If you have the time to do a review, you can add it to an author's page where you purchased this book as well as other online review outlets.

You can find all of my books here http://maxinedouglasauthor.blogspot.com (Hot Sexy Stories) and more about the Blue Moon Magic series at http://ourbluemoonworld.blogspot.com/.

Thank you so much for reading, and for spending time with me.

In gratitude,

Debi Wilder